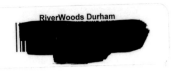

D0802441

Cold Sunflowers

Mark Sippings

Cover design by Design for Writers

ISBN 978-1-9999362-0-4 (Paperback)
ISBN 978-1-9999362-1-1 (Ebook)

For Eleanor and Poppy

PROLOGUE

1972

The street lights flickered, shrouded in the mist that swirled around them.

There was a hum in the air, a crackle of electricity that seeped into the pores of the two men as they stood at the top of the gently sloping hill.

They were in a residential area. Rows of neatly cut lawns fronted the houses and edged the road. In the driveways, cars waiting for the morning's journey stood idle. An occasional light illuminated a window, turning out the night and throwing a yellow glow across the pavement.

But mostly the dark prevailed with stars able to pinprick the sky.

The men's breath, heavy with excitement, emulated the mist, blurring the tiny specks of light. The two were close together now, one slightly stooped, the other upright. They seemed out of place, oblivious to the end-of-summer chill and in no hurry to find the warmth of their homes.

Rain began to fall, silver on the road, dancing around their feet in the streetlight.

They laughed; the slimmer man raised his head. The rain fell on his eyelids, into his open mouth and on to his tongue. He turned on the spot, face towards the sky. He was young. Longish dark hair, devoid of style, hid his eyes. He wore a black duffel coat, jeans and desert boots.

The other raised his arms Christ-like, palms upwards to catch the rain. The lamplight accentuated the whiteness of his wavy hair and it was easy to see he was older. He wore black formal trousers and a white quilted overcoat. His shoes were sensible but worn and scuffed. He was not someone who worried unduly about his appearance.

He smiled, then spoke. A whisper.

'Are you ready? It's the closest you'll get to flying without leaving the ground.'

The reply was laced with excitement though barely audible above the hiss of the dancing rain.

'Show me.'

The older man lowered his arms, reached into his coat pocket and pulled out a small round object. He caressed it between his thumb and forefinger. After so many years the movement of his circling thumb was as natural as blinking.

It was a French franc, battered and brown, its long history evident in the smoothness of its surface.

'Follow it down the hill. Go as quickly as your legs will take you. Leap whenever you can and don't stop even if you overtake it.'

The younger man looked down the slope, poised, legs bent in a runner's starting position, arms prepared to pump.

In a well-practised routine, his older companion swung his arm back and, in a movement so smooth it belied his age, sent the coin upwards in a perfect arc, then rolling and bouncing down the hill.

The younger man chased after it. He was no athlete and his legs and arms flailed awkwardly as he raced down the slope. His head tilted at a strange angle and the older man smiled as his companion gained momentum.

He was now going so fast his legs could barely keep up with him. He heard nothing but the breeze and the sound of his footsteps pounding the pavement. Then he leapt, arms outstretched, and everything was quiet for the briefest of moments. He landed lightly and ran faster still. The street lights, the stars and the pavement merged into a mist-filled swirl that almost overwhelmed him.

Eyes closed, mouth open, gasping with joy, he ran and leapt, overtaking the franc that had now fallen on its side.

And then it was over.

He was at the bottom of the hill, hands on his knees, panting heavily. He straightened, raised his arms to the stars and jumped, laughing and whooping.

The older man walked down the hill towards the franc. Lost in thought, he bent slowly to pick it up, passed it between his fingers and warmed it in his hands.

'Come on. You do it. You must – please, you must.' The younger man's voice cut through the silence.

'I can't. I'm past all that. How did it feel?'

'Like I was the wind! Please do it.'

Smiling, the older man looked at the coin and once more sent it rolling down the hill. He ran after it, stuttering on stiff legs until magically, his momentum, fuelled by the hill and gravity, began to increase and in an act of grace and wonder, he leapt ...

CHAPTER ONE
The Fish

1917

He leapt …

The noise was deafening, thudding his heart. The zing and whistle of bullets made him wince and watch the world through eyes squeezed shut in a smile of despair.

An explosion twenty yards away knocked him off his feet. He landed heavily, arms covering his head, unworried that he'd buried his face in the mud and was choking on dirty brown water.

One beautiful summer's day, when he was a child, he had caught a fish. He was so proud of his catch that he'd wanted to show his parents and had run home from the river, stopping at every muddy puddle to let the slippery silver creature fight for life. How many puddles had there been? How many writhing gulps until the struggle had become too great and all was still?

Now, here in the mud, it was he who was drowning, retching, fingers clawing for life in the oozing mud. Yet all the while an inner voice tempted him to lie still, to sleep, to give up the struggle.

He turned his head just as the debris from the explosion showered him, filling his eyes and mouth with mud, wood, cotton, flesh and blood. Wide-eyed and gasping the smoke-filled air, he scrambled to his feet and rested his back against the wall of the shell hole. Another explosion left him unable to hear or see. He fumbled for a large wooden box, pulled it closer and wrapped his body around it, cocooning it as more mud and debris crashed from the sky.

He screamed an animal prayer of spit and snot, but heard nothing above the cacophony. He tried to stand but his legs would no longer carry his weight and he dropped to his knees.

It was then, when the world was about to break, that he felt a hand on his shoulder, pulling him. He turned, and there was a blackened, weather-beaten face and a mouth working, moving ... talking?

'Ernest.' A whisper.

'Ernie.' Louder.

'Ernest!' A shout.

'Get up. NOW.'

The hand moved from his shoulder, took a second box and slammed it against the muddy wall until the glass inside rattled. Then half-walking, half-sliding, the two men stumbled back through the clawing, sucking mud to their trench.

* * *

The soldiers sat on wooden benches, their backs against the muddy trench wall. The sun was high in the sky and all was quiet apart from the birdsong that pierced the unfamiliar silence. Ernest squinted into the blue, his hands covering his eyes against the sun.

He was the youngest, and looked barely sixteen – dark wavy hair, a smooth white face that had never seen a razor, and in the shadow of his raised hand inquisitive bright-blue eyes that surveyed his surroundings, darting from face to face. The uniform, supplied to him in England, was too big; the quartermaster's prediction that he'd grow into it would take a long time to realise. On his lap sat a battered oblong box which he would open at every opportunity – much to the consternation of his comrades – and with his thumb and forefinger slide out a black, bellowed camera.

The men took drags from tiny roll-ups, the smoke rising above them, hazing the sky. They were too tired to talk. Ernest leaned against his companion.

'Thanks, Bill,' he said.

'You're okay, Ernie. I told you stick with me, mate; you'll be all right. You're a dope!'

He playfully pushed Ernest, causing discontented mutterings amongst the men.

'Watch it!'

'Grow up.'

'Bloody idiots.'

Bill raised his eyebrows and a smile touched his

weather-beaten face. In contrast to Ernest's, his shirt stretched over a muscular chest.

'Bill, I don't have much left. In the hole I felt like sleeping. I ... I didn't want to get up.'

'Mate, we'll be home soon. Remember, everything happens for a reason. I told you, we're going to be the bigwigs when this war is over and you're going to take pictures of the rich and famous when they visit Bill's restaurant.'

Ernest nodded and laughed, a single hesitant sound. He looked down at his boots, crossed one leg over the other, gripped the heel and with a slow painful movement tried to ease it off. The boot remained firmly in place. He groaned, perspiration beading on his face, frustration boiling over. Tears burned behind his closed eyelids.

Bill rose from his seat and knelt in front of Ernest.

'Come on mate. Let me,' he said quietly.

Ernest leant back, his mouth tight, his eyes closed and wet.

Bill, oblivious to the mud that coated his fingers and seeped through his thick woollen uniform, took hold of each boot and slowly pulled it off. Then, gentle as a mother, he rolled Ernest's sodden green socks down to his ankles and eased them over his painful swollen feet, avoiding the raw red and yellow blisters.

For the first time in a fortnight, Ernest felt the sun on his feet. His breath caught in his chest; a shuddering gasp. He lowered them slowly to the wooden boards and wiggled his toes, marvelling that such an act of kindness could fill his heart with life again.

CHAPTER TWO

The Photograph

1972

He lowered pale, wizened feet to the floorboards. Blue veins meandered around his ankles towards the tiny purple blood vessels that coloured his heels. His toenails were thick and white.

Sunlight shafted through the gap in the curtains, highlighting the dust motes that swooped and swirled around his feet.

An occasional damp patch darkened the patterned wallpaper, which in the corner of the room had peeled away from the coving. A yellow candlewick bedspread lay ruffled and forgotten to one side of the double bed. Two bedside cabinets in a buttery faux marble had seen better days. A single glass of water stood untouched on one.

Photographs adorned the matching chest of drawers. A wedding – the bride and groom, heads touching, knife shared, about to cut the lower section of a three-tier cake. An elderly lady with a kind smile, her white hair immaculately set – she sat in a garden on an upholstered, high-backed blue chair, surrounded by tubs of flowering geraniums and Busy Lizzies; a peach tree behind her framed the scene. Next to that, a smaller photograph – a young man standing next to a gleaming white headstone; yellow roses climbed about it. And at the front, a larger picture – the seaside. The sky blue and perfect. Two older people, still in love, standing hand in hand on the beach. To the left of them and in the distance, a large dark rock formation rose from the sea. Waves washed through a natural arch in the rock, releasing foamy white seahorses. The man was smiling and offering the woman chips hidden in newspaper that billowed upwards towards the circling seagulls.

It was an old-fashioned room.

Tired.

It was as though the bubbles of energy and excitement that had once sparkled and fizzed had gone flat.

The man felt the same. He was tired too.

The endless monotony – saucepans boiling on the small four-ringed cooker in the kitchen, potato peelings, ready-made meals. And, oh, Sunday. Please, no more Sundays.

Getting out of the house felt like visiting time in a hospital – something to be looked forward to no matter how mundane – and the man used every opportunity to leave his home.

But he was not looking forward to today's outing.

Where had he put that book?

Why was he feeling so old lately?

Where had the world of his childhood gone? The dragons, the princes, the knights and, above all, the honour? Yes, where was that these days? He wanted the world to cradle him, to make him warm and comfortable again, but he wished to be worthy of its embrace. He'd been falling for a while, knew he must stand up again, but his old legs hurt and sometimes he thought it might be easier just to lie down, go to sleep and never get up. Ah that old memory again …

'Fight it. Fight it.' He smiled. 'Everything happens for a reason.'

He showered quickly, quietly humming a catchy but unknown tune he'd heard on the radio. He dried himself and moved to the sink, toothbrush in hand. Steam had misted the mirror and he wiped his smudged reflection with a towel. Piercing blue eyes stared back, still the intense gaze of a youthful seventeen-year-old. At least they hadn't changed. Many people said his lined face made him look distinguished, but he hated that word – it was just a nice way of saying he looked old. He was proud that his appearance belied his age though, and he ran his fingers through his thick, slightly curled and swept-back white hair. He smiled again and laughter lines etched his face.

The toaster pinged as the kettle came to the boil. Butter, marmalade, milk, teabag – the old routine. He sipped at his steaming mug and slowly ate his toast. He'd put a small spoonful of marmalade and butter on the side of his plate so he could flavour each mouthful, just the way his wife used to.

He grinned, picked up the paper and began reading; always from the back, always the sport first.

Breakfast eaten, he walked to the hall, pulled on his white anorak and opened the front door. Light streamed in, bathing the hall table in misty yellow. He looked down at a lone photograph haloed by the light – a young, beautiful woman, her dark hair tied back, wearing a white blouse open at the neck. She was laughing. The picture looked old and was fading.

He ran a finger down the frame before stepping outside and closing the door firmly behind him.

CHAPTER THREE

The Lost Giro

Raymond curled tightly under the cosy blankets, knees pulled to his chest. He was eighteen, slightly built, verging on skinny, with a pale face surrounded by longish dark, lank hair.

The early-morning sun was bright against the thin brown curtains, which swayed gently as his room breathed in the outside air through the open window. Occasionally a car could be heard from the road.

He clasped his hands together in front of his mouth and closed his eyes. His lips moved in silent prayer.

'Gentle Jesus, meek and mild, look upon a little child. Pity my simplicity. Suffer me to come to thee. God bless Mum, Dad, nannies, granddads, aunties, uncles, cousins John and Clive, all kind friends, and make Ray a good boy, for Jesus' sake. And, Lord, thank you for all the things you've done for me. Amen.' He closed his eyes tighter, the lids wrinkling. 'And please, Lord, please make it come this morning. Twenty prayers tonight if it comes this morning, I promise, Lord. Jesus, Holy Ghost, please help – please make it come. God bless. Amen. Oh, and PS, I'm really sorry I forgot to say my prayers last night.'

The letter box clattered. Raymond heard his mother move from the kitchen, into the hallway and up to the front door. He closed his eyes, crossed his fingers and whispered, 'Pleeease make it be here.'

'Raymond,' she called. 'Ray, it hasn't come. Get up. You'll have to go down there now.'

He heard her begin to climb the stairs.

'Ray, do you hear me?'

Another step.

'RAYMOND!' She sounded exasperated.

He pulled the bed covers over his head and kicked his legs up and down in frustration, cursing quietly.

'Bollocks, bollocks, bollocks.' He took a deep breath and composed himself. 'Okay, Mum.'

He picked up a book from his bedside cabinet. The cover was decorated with towering yellow sunflowers whose enormous flowering heads partially obscured a golden orb. The pages were dog-eared and folded in several places. He flicked through, found a marked page and began to read. After only a few words he shook his head and threw the book down on to the bed.

He got up quickly and pulled on his skinny jeans and baggy T-shirt, then made use of the hairbrush his mum had given him shortly after he started senior school.

He remembered that day clearly.

He hated school dinners so had rushed home for lunch.

On the dining-room table was a brown paper bag. He'd opened it and been surprised by the turquoise hairbrush with black bendy teeth. He had no idea why that brush meant so much to him. Such a mundane object, but it was special. It showed his mum cared. She had noticed him struggling to comb his tangled, lengthening hair and had found a solution.

He turned and looked at his reflection in the full-length mirror on the far wall of his bedroom.

He didn't like his appearance.

There was no doubt about it – the primary-school nickname of Skinny Ribs, although cruel, was quite justified. The baggy T-shirt concealed his body, but the short sleeves exposed his arms – long, thin, devoid of muscle. He moved closer to the mirror, examining the whiteness of his face. Another spot had nudged through, the reddened skin matching his equally sore-looking eyelids.

He yanked the hairbrush through the tangles. As always, his hair curled at a peculiar angle above his ear so that even his mum's hairspray struggled to flatten it. When his fringe refused to comply, he saw with horror that it had become a matted lacquered lump.

It was too late for a hair wash, so he wandered down the stairs and into the kitchen.

His dad had recently decorated the wall around the sink with orange tiles and then, pleased with his work, had extended the tiling to below the wooden cabinets. The rest of the room was a lemon yellow and Raymond was still unconvinced that the two colours complemented one another, although his dad insisted the look was modern.

From the kitchen sink, the front garden and the road were visible. Raymond would often stand there daydreaming when he should have been washing up.

The previous evening his dad had said he'd be taking a 'Whitley' in the morning – a day off when you weren't really sick – but Raymond was still surprised when he saw his father sitting at the oversized kitchen table.

His dad held a large newspaper in one hand, folded in half, and a piece of toast in the other. The front-page story had captured his attention but he glanced up and smiled as Raymond nudged past him and sat down.

His dad was handsome, well built, but not overweight. He wore his black hair swept backwards, like a film star's, and his chiselled chin was appropriately accented with a Kirk Douglas dimple.

Raymond envied his dad's physique and, as always, involuntarily looked down at his own body.

His mother was at the sink, drying the plates left on the draining board from the previous evening. She wore a red dressing gown pulled tightly around her and fastened with a cord. It set off her short dark perm.

'What are you having, Ray? You can get the 10.05 if you hurry.' Her voice was cheery and kind, and she always spoke with a smile.

'Just some toast, please. I'll go later. I was going to sort the garden out this morning.'

His dad took a precise bite from his toast. He was a kind, caring man but had old-fashioned values and kept emotion well and truly bottled – the English way. Unlike his wife, he was usually quiet, rarely excited. A black-and-white photo next to her coloured one. But the two complemented each other and seldom had a cross word.

'Your flowers won't give your mum her housekeeping.'

'Oh, Dad, I hate the dole office.' Raymond could hear himself whining. 'Let me leave it one more day. I'll definitely go tomorrow.'

His dad put the paper down and looked directly at Raymond.

'Ray, you're entitled to that money. And, honestly, I'm fed up with you moping around. You need a job. I'll take you to London on Friday; there's plenty of jobs up there.'

Raymond's mum, as if sensing an argument, turned towards them from the sink.

'I'll get something soon, Dad. I will.' Raymond felt his temper building. 'You get up every day at six in the morning and don't get home until eight. I never see you. I don't want to do that.'

His dad lay a piece of toast on the plate. Raymond sensed the lecture before it began.

'Look, Ray, life isn't easy. Most of us do jobs we don't like just to pay the bills. I've told you since you were little, do something you enjoy. But you don't seem to want to do anything. There's a tiny minority of people earning a bloody fortune doing something they like, you know – snooker players or footballers. The rest of us just earn a pittance.'

Raymond was breathing heavily now. He raised his eyebrows and shook his head.

'I know, Dad – you've told me a million times,' he replied, his tone mocking.

His father stopped chewing and glared. Raymond felt the heat rise to his cheeks, then shame as tears formed, the lump in his throat growing bigger. As if sensing Raymond's discomfort his dad spoke gently.

'Ray, I want you to be unique. I never wanted you to be part of the majority, but that's the way it is sometimes. Pop down to the dole office and see what's happening.'

Raymond's mum put a mug of tea on to the table in front of him. He picked it up and sipped slowly, occasionally blowing on to the surface. His eyes stung. He stared ahead, saying nothing; sure his quivering voice would betray his feelings. He noticed his mum look over at her husband and shake her head. *Enough.* She passed Raymond a piece of toast and he bit the corner half-heartedly.

His parents looked at him, no doubt wondering what had become of their once bright, bubbly boy. When had the shadow descended and dragged him into a colourless world?

His mum looked up, as if stung into action.

'Ray! I know – why don't I come with you?'

Raymond's head jerked up and he rose from his seat.

'Mum, no!' he squeaked.

'Ray, we love you,' his mum said softly, 'but we worry about you. You stay in your room. You don't talk to us and you seem so sad. Have a look at your flowers and then get the 11.30 if you like.'

Raymond's breath caught in his throat and he gulped.

'Okay, Mum.'

Toast in hand, he made his way back to his bedroom.

CHAPTER FOUR

Cold Sunflowers

Raymond's home was part of a new estate. A long row of identical houses stood side by side, white horizontal boards cladding the top of each one and all shielded from the rain and the sun by the same sloping roofs and black guttering. Only the front gardens nosing the pavement displayed their owners' individuality. Raymond's parents had built a small wall around their front lawn, dug borders and planted shrubs; the garden looked mature and planned.

Raymond walked over to several straggly flowers tied with green string to bamboo poles, which were more than twice the height of the plants.

It was sunny and aside from the shadows cast by the occasional shrub or bush, most of the garden was bathed in yellow. Raymond's flowers were in the shade, hidden against the wall of the house. The drab location reflected their lack of vitality. Their leaves were small, pale and feeble and despite the valiant efforts of the string and the pole, the stems leaned forward, craving sunlight.

Raymond lovingly dug the soil around the plants, removed weeds and dead leaves and tried in vain to get them to stand at ninety degrees.

He picked up the book he had tried to read in his bedroom.

> *Sunflowers will grow approximately six inches a week during the summer, reaching a height of over six feet. Shoots and large green leaves will amply cover a long stem and a glorious head will form after about nine weeks ...*

He put the book back down on the grass, shook his head and used the watering can to drench the dry earth around each flower. He sighed and looked at his watch, stared once more at the plants, willing them to grow, and hurriedly took the tools and book to the shed. After one more check to assure himself he'd packed everything away, he walked up the garden path and on to the road. It was 11.20 a.m.

CHAPTER FIVE

The Bus Ride

The 11.30 was packed.

People stood two abreast in the gangway, grimly gripping the vertical poles that rose from the back of every other seat, steadying themselves as the bus stopped, started, twisted and turned.

The smoke from a dozen cigarettes drifted close to the ceiling and hung there, blurring the advertisements above the windows. Raymond always read these hoping to make the time pass a little quicker.

Today he'd been lucky. He had caught the bus at an earlier stop and found a seat on the lower deck next to an elderly lady. She'd looked friendly enough, but frowned and tutted when she realised she'd have to move her shopping bag.

Sometimes it seemed that a seat was more trouble than it was worth, and as the bus became crowded, he felt the standing passengers' questioning eyes on him.

Had he deserved that seat?

Should he give it up?

There were older people standing but would they be offended if he offered to swap?

As for the women, he was sure that the new Women's Lib movement didn't even want doors opened for its members, let alone the gift of a seat.

It was all so confusing and added to his unease.

The bus was a double-decker – the worst type. Dark red with a grey trim above the windows. The new design, with the front entrance enclosed by sliding doors, meant he couldn't leap off if he felt the need. A tiny cockpit ensconced the driver at the front while the conductor patrolled the aisles.

Today's conductor was a middle-aged woman, mid-to-late forties, so a little older than his mother. She had longish auburn hair, wavy rather than curly. Her face was tight and her lips thin. She didn't suffer fools – Raymond had seen her push a young boy off a crowded bus because he'd had the audacity to ask whether she was going to a stop only a few miles down the road.

Around her neck she bore a heavy silver ticket machine. Turning the tiny black handle produced a sound of whizzing gears and a flimsy white ticket. A large leather money bag was laid flat on a raised thigh and opened as she leant against an adjacent seat. She'd shake the bag vigorously to produce the correct change.

Raymond hated bus trips; it was not so much the journey as the getting-off. He never had the courage to ring the bell or pull the wire on the older buses, relying on the conductor to do it for him. On several occasions he had missed his stop because she'd been upstairs.

Panic rose in his chest and, with it, the familiar shortness of breath, irregular heartbeat, and fear that he would collapse and die.

It was the same with every trip. He rubbed anxiously at his chest – up, down, faster and faster – in a feeble attempt to keep his heart going. Several times he inadvertently nudged the woman next to him but he was oblivious to her discomfort until she pointedly stared at him with raised eyebrows.

'Sorry,' he whispered, and quickly focused his gaze on his knees.

The bus was about to arrive at the stop before his and he looked out of the window at the waiting queue, trying to gauge whether anyone would head upstairs. Youngsters seemed to regard the top deck as their domain while older people more often than not took the lower. Today was a mixed bag.

He turned his attention to the conductor, then lowered his head once more and closed his eyes.

'Stay here. Please stay here,' he whispered. 'Please, God, don't let anyone else go upstairs; let the conductor stay down here. Twenty prayers tonight if she stays. I'm on the sixty-five going towards town. Gentle Jesus, please help. Amen.'

The bus slowed to a halt and several people got on. They looked to the right, saw passengers standing in the aisle and climbed the stairs.

Raymond groaned loudly.

'Oh, bollocks.'

Several people looked around to see who'd uttered the remark. Raymond shrank into his seat and stared at the small red button, the words *Push Once* moulded into the shiny steel surround.

Familiar roads drifted past the window and he sensed his stop nearing. The conductor was nowhere to be seen although the whirr of the ticket machine and clatter of coins could be heard.

Raymond felt the tension in his chest mount. He breathed deeply but it was as if the oxygen couldn't reach his lungs. He tried again this time almost panting. Sometimes poking his tongue over his bottom lip while rubbing his chest helped, but not today.

His elderly neighbour looked at him, concerned. Her gaze moved across the aisle to another passenger who shrugged.

Raymond clutched the thin silver rail of the seat in front and tried to steady himself. Two seats ahead, a man lifted his bag. Was he reaching for the bell? Raymond's heart leapt, but the passenger merely adjusted his sitting position, put his bag on his lap and rummaged through it.

The stop was approaching fast; only two hundred yards. Raymond looked around again, his breathing even shallower, certain his heart would explode. He felt the tickle of perspiration on his cheek.

The bus pushed onwards, doggedly eating up the road. Raymond stared at the bell. He just needed to stand up, move forward and press it.

Fifty yards until the stop. None of the passengers had moved. Raymond gripped the seat in front of him and pulled himself upright. His legs trembled as he took a step towards the bell. Timorously, he reached forward, trying to control his shaking hand.

'Are you all right? Can I help you?' said a female voice.

Before Raymond could answer, the conductor pirouetted down the stairs and, using the handrail to adjust her position, swung on to the front platform. She saw him edging forward, reached up and pushed the bell beside her. The bus came to a juddering halt.

Raymond fumbled past the standing passengers.

'Excuse me,' he muttered, and they moved aside reluctantly, each of them eying his empty seat and calculating the age and sex of their companions.

As he neared the exit, he mumbled a thank-you to the conductor and hopped off.

He stood on the pavement and watched the bus disappear around a corner. His racing heart slowed and he inhaled deeply, comforted as the warm air filled his lungs. He skipped for a few paces, then stopped, horrified when he realised what he was doing. He looked up. The cloudy sky was turning blue, and a bubble of relief burst from within and formed into the widest of smiles.

'Thank you, Lord. Twenty prayers tonight.'

* * *

The queue for the DHSS snaked out the door and stretched down the concrete steps. Several people lay on the grass in front of the building, soaking up the sun. Large cans of Special Brew littered the surrounding area.

Raymond hated going to the social – loathed the grey, characterless building and the mundane questions. But most of all it was that sense of feeling like a child beside his streetwise companions with their jokes, their shoving and their swearing. He knew in his heart that everyone around him wasn't like that, but it was as if he were a magnet for these individuals and more than once a visit to the dole office had resulted in an embarrassing altercation.

The queue inched forward until Raymond finally entered the harsh, neon-lit building and took a small, white, dog-eared card with the number sixty-three written on it in black marker pen.

He looked around.

Glass-fronted booths lined one side of the room. On the walls, torn and graffiti covered posters hung at odd angles, their corners discoloured and lumpy. People milled about and chatted; it seemed unorganised and unhurried, and the atmosphere was filled with a sense of hopeless acceptance.

Occasionally he'd hear a voice, raised and desperate, or the thud of a desk being slammed before someone hurriedly left the building, eyes bulging, daring anyone to look at them.

Raymond eyed a row of red plastic chairs secured to the floor. He spotted an empty seat at the end and sat down. Opposite was an elderly man wearing a light quilted anorak, his white hair swept back. He looked out of place amid the noisy throng. He smiled at Raymond, who quickly looked down at his shoes.

'Fifty-nine.' The number crackled through the loudspeaker.

The elderly man glanced at his card, stood up and walked over to the empty booth. Raymond watched as he sat down, then strained to listen to the conversation, hoping he'd pick up some tips for his own interview.

'Good afternoon,' said the man to the clerk.

'Hello. How can I help you today?'

'Well, I seem to have lost my order book and I have no money left in the house at all.'

'Oh, I'm sorry to hear that. And you've no idea where it could be?'

'No. I feel so stupid – it's just disappeared.'

'Not to worry. Could I have your name and national insurance number, please?'

'Yes, Ernest Gardiner, and the number is BG752036D.'

The clerk recorded the details on a sheet of white paper.

'Thank you, Mr Gardiner. I'll just go and find your papers and then I'll have a word with my supervisor and we'll see what we can do. I won't keep you too long.'

Raymond felt a hard nudge on his arm.

'It's your turn, mate. Hurry up.'

'Final call, sixty-three.' The words hissed through the speakers.

'Thanks,' mumbled Raymond. He shuffled towards the booth, self-consciously looking around at the waiting people, and sat in front of the glass screen. The clerk was a young man, probably not that much older than him. He thought of his dad's words about finding a job.

'Hello. How can I help today?'

'Hello, um, my giro hasn't come. It should have come last week but ... but I've waited and waited and nothing's arrived.'

'I see. Has the post come today?'

'Yes.'

'The second post?'

Raymond hesitated.

'Well, no, but the giro was supposed to come last week.'

In the next booth the elderly man was waiting patiently; he gave Raymond a reassuring smile.

'I see,' said the clerk. 'Well, where are you currently living?'

'With my mum and dad.'

'So you're single, with no dependants and a non-householder. Is that right?'

Raymond began to feel uncomfortable; he could tell by the clerk's tone that the conversation wasn't going the way he wanted.

'Yes, that's right. I live with my mum and dad, but I have no money and I, ah, I owe my mum twenty pounds.'

'I see. Unfortunately, I won't be able to replace the giro for seven weeks. I have to send your details to our office in Ireland. They'll do a search to see if your giro's been cashed; if nothing comes back within seven weeks, I can replace it. Now, if you'll take this form, fill it in over there on the counter and drop it back through the letter box, I can get a search going.' The clerk slid the sheet under the glass screen and towards Raymond.

'But ... but I have no money. I owe my mum.'

'Sorry, Mr ...?'

'It's Mann, Raymond Mann.'

'Sorry, Mr Mann, but as you're single, a non-house-holder, living with your parents, there's no hardship involved and you'll have to wait for your money.'

'B-But my mum won't believe me. She won't believe I've even been here. Can you write me a note, please?'

'Sorry, Mr Mann.' The clerk sighed. 'Now, I have other people to see. If there's nothing else, just fill in this form and I'll contact you in about seven weeks.'

The clerk in the booth next to Raymond returned to his desk and began talking to the elderly man. Raymond looked across at them.

'Okay, I've spoken to my supervisor and what we can do is give you two weeks' money. That should tide you over until your replacement book is ready. Obviously if the old one turns up you must return it straight away,' he said.

'Thank you,' replied the man. 'You've been so kind.'

Raymond sat spellbound by the conversation. A tapping on the glass screen in front of him brought him out of his trance.

'Mr Mann, if there's nothing else, I have other people to see.'

Raymond got up from the seat and trudged towards the exit at an all-time low. Why was everything against him?

Then his name boomed from the speakers.

'Mr Mann, Mr Mann, please return to the desk.'

Three youths sniggered as Raymond retraced his steps to the booth.

'Mr Mann, you forgot to take your form. Fill it in and pop it in the post box,' said the clerk.

'Okay. Thank you,' said Raymond quietly.

He walked to the exit again.

The three youths whispered to each other and laughed loudly. One, a skinhead with dark-blue tattoos down his arms, looked directly at Raymond.

'All right, Mr Mann,' he said menacingly. 'How's Mr Bendy, or should we say Mr Bender?' Hoots of laughter ensued. Other people turned to look and were smiling.

Raymond's cheeks grew hot and he knew a telltale blush was forming. He tried to hurry past.

'Excuse me,' he said assertively, in a vain attempt to hide his discomfort.

A second, stockier youth reached forward and tried to grab Raymond's leg.

'Has Miss Tickle been up to no good?'

There was more laughter as the youths leaned back in their seats and stuck their legs out, bridging the aisle and blocking Raymond's way.

He dodged an outstretched hand and attempted to hop over the legs. The youths raised their limbs when he was halfway across. Tight, faded blue jeans and black Doctor Martens formed a treacherous obstacle course that adjusted to his every move.

Laughter filled the office as he struggled astride the legs. He felt the other claimants' eyes boring into his back. Embarrassment burned through him.

At last he escaped and hurried out into the fresh air. He sat on a brick wall running along the office boundary and completed the form, balancing it awkwardly on his skinny thigh, then posted it in the letter box by the front entrance.

He returned to the wall, sat down heavily and put his head in his hands.

'Jesus, I know you didn't make it come,' he whispered, 'but let it come tomorrow. Please, Lord, thirty prayers if it comes tomorrow. Promise. Amen.'

The sun was high in the sky and Raymond tilted his head back, letting the hot rays bathe his face. What now? He couldn't tell his mum; she'd never believe him.

Raymond lowered his head. The elderly man who'd been in the next booth ambled past and nodded.

There was a shout from the doorway.

'There he is – it's Mr Mann. And, look, he's got his mate Mr Bender with him.' The three youths from the dole office made a beeline for Raymond. As they strolled towards him they laughed and pushed one another, mimicking gay courtesans.

'Are you two off to do some DIY, or did you get a bum-hole plumbing course from the social?'

They circled Raymond and the elderly man. One moved forward. He cracked his knuckles and flexed the muscles in his arms. Raymond looked around for an escape route. The older man just smiled and turned to face the group.

'What's wrong? I'm sure this can all be sorted out amicably,' he said politely.

The skinhead pressed his face up close to the pensioner's. 'Amicably wankibly, you old poofter. Shut up.' Spit sprayed on to the older man's face.

The skinhead bounced back and stood in line with his

grinning accomplices, then spoke softly. 'Listen, Mr Mann and Mr Bender, we're a bit skint – you know how it is. So if you have some loose change we'll show our appreciation by ... NOT SMASHING YOUR FUCKIN' FACES IN.'

Raymond and the old man jumped back in fright and the three youths burst into laughter again. Raymond, pale and shaking, put his hand into his pocket while the old man retrieved a large juicy orange from his carrier bag.

'We don't want no fuckin' food, you fuckin' idiot,' the lead skinhead shouted, spit again erupting from his mouth.

The older man smiled and looked at the orange. 'Oh, what a waste,' he whispered, then threw it hard into the face of the skinhead.

The yob fell to the ground, clutching his head and rolling around while his companions tried to lift him.

'What's wrong with you people? Where's your pride? Grow up,' the old man said calmly. He turned to Raymond. 'Come on. Let's get a coffee.'

Raymond stood still and open-mouthed as the elderly man marched away, his back straight and his head high.

The yobs huddled around their fallen friend. 'We'll report you – you could have blinded him, you fucking bender.'

The man stopped, looked back at the youths and smiled, their V-signs making no impression on him.

'I can see the headlines now. "Frail old man beats three thugs with an orange." I don't think so, do you? What will your friends think of the fearsome threesome?' He glanced at Raymond. 'Would you like a drink?' he said kindly.

'Er ... yes. Yes please,' Raymond replied, his voice small and shaking. He jogged to catch up.

The pair walked in silence through the grey concrete underpass that shielded them from the newly opened dual carriageway. The drone of traffic rumbled above them. They crossed the old link road and entered the throng of shoppers. The older man seemed sure of his destination and Raymond often had to double his stride or do an awkward step to keep up.

They reached a small cafe called The Salt Shaker. Ernest pushed open the single red door and gestured for Raymond to enter. A bell jangled as he walked through and a well-spoken man with longish curly hair and a moustache welcomed them inside.

'Morning, Ernest. The usual?'

'Yes, please. And one for my friend here.'

Raymond had noticed The Salt Shaker when shopping with his mum; he'd assumed it just sold takeaway burgers and something foreign called chilli con carne. Now he saw two tiny tables set beside the wall, each covered by a blue floral tablecloth.

'Take a seat,' said the proprietor. 'I'll bring them over to you.'

'Thanks, Keith,' said Ernest, walking over to the furthest table. He pulled out a chair, sat down and beckoned Raymond to join him.

Raymond looked around the coffee shop. It was small but the white walls gave the illusion of space. In front of Keith was a large silver bain-marie and Raymond wondered if this contained the mysterious chilli con carne. To the side of the owner was a greasy, well-used iron griddle for the burgers, and behind him, a spot lit blackboard displaying the price list. The thick chalk handwriting flowed and swirled artistically over the surface.

The old man offered Raymond his hand.

'Hello, I'm Ernest Gardiner. Pleased to meet you.'

Raymond accepted the man's hand tentatively. It felt cold, a little bony and fragile.

'I'm Raymond, Raymond Mann,' he said quietly.

Ernest seemed agitated.

'I ask you, what makes people do that, Raymond? Why is everyone so angry? People's rudeness is just extraordinary. We have a wonderful country, yet they live like that and get enjoyment from someone else's misfortune. I tell you, Raymond ...'

Keith appeared with their coffees.

'Here we are, gents,' he said. He looked at Raymond and smiled. 'If I were you I'd drink that quickly and get going.' He pointed a thumb over his shoulder towards the door. 'Otherwise you'll get the thoughts of Chairman Ernie for the next three hours. I'm a captive audience, but don't let him snare you as well.'

Keith spoke with authority and a quiet charm. His voice was neither high class nor accented, but it demanded to be heard. Raymond envied the man's natural confidence and seemingly effortless conversational skills.

Ernest laughed. 'Yes and you, Mr Worth, will be the first against the wall come the revolution.'

Keith placed two white plastic cups on the table. Raymond reached forward and picked his up but it was hot and burnt his fingers. He quickly put it down, hoping no one had noticed.

Ernest was still laughing. 'Yes, it's not the most luxurious of places, I'm afraid. I don't know why I keep coming back! Hmm, maybe it's the company.' He raised his cup to Keith in a mock toast. Keith waved a single finger and touched his temple in a friendly salute.

They drank their coffee slowly. Raymond concentrated on each sip, searching for something interesting to say but finding himself mute.

Ernest broke the silence. 'I'm so sorry about losing my temper like that. We don't even know each other but it makes me so cross. All the chances in the world and they choose to be like that. Anyway, enough. Tell me what you like to do.'

Raymond felt even more uneasy. His dad's words about finding a job echoed in his head. What would this old man think if he found out he was unemployed? He slid his chair backwards.

'Thanks for your help but I've got to go. I've just this minute remembered my mum's expecting me. I'm really, really sorry. Thanks again for the coffee and everything. Bye bye. Hope to see you again sometime.'

'Oh, don't leave,' Ernest quickly replied. 'You haven't drunk your coffee yet. I can give you a lift home if you like; that'll save you some time. I have my car. I'm just a silly old man who doesn't get out much. Well, apart from The Salt Shaker, of course, which doesn't really count.' He looked over at Keith and smiled. 'You know ...' He leaned back in his chair and linked his fingers high on his chest.

'I long for the days of chivalry and honour, which I suspect weren't there in the first place. In my cranky old brain and with my rose-coloured spectacles on, everything old seems better, and I wish it wasn't so. What I need is for someone to show me I'm wrong.'

'But I have to get my bus,' Raymond said hurriedly. He felt odd. 'My mum's waiting for me.'

'Finish your coffee and I'll take you home in the car.'

'But ... but I don't know you, and my mum's waiting for me; she'll be wondering where I am.' Raymond had decided to emphasise his mum just in case the old man was planning to kidnap him. Then, intrigued, he asked, 'Can you see without your glasses?'

'Pardon?' asked Ernest, puzzled. 'What glasses?'

'Your rose ones,' Raymond replied. 'I haven't seen any like that. Are they like John Lennon's?' He picked up his coffee cup and took a sip, eager to hear the answer.

Ernest laughed, a gentle rumble that wrapped Raymond in its warmth.

'Oh, yes, they're very special, but I wear them far too much,' he said. 'Raymond, I understand why you're reluctant to accept a lift home from me; I'm an elderly man whom you've never met before. But this is what I mean about the world today – I'm just offering to give you a ride home in my car. It's a simple act of kindness but these days it suddenly has lots of different connotations. You know what? A little boy fell over in front of me the other day. I went to pick him up but then changed my mind in case his mother thought I was about to molest him. What's happening to the world, Raymond?' Ernest took a large mouthful of coffee and then tipped the cup back. 'A great friend of mine once said that everything happens for a reason. You seem a little down. Maybe the reason we met was so we could cheer each other up. I really hope so.' He stood. 'My car's just down the road. If you'd like a lift, you'll be most welcome. And if not, it's been wonderful talking to you. I'm sure that when you get to my age, you too will have some rose-coloured spectacles of your very own.'

Ernest paid the bill, said goodbye to Keith, and smiled briefly at Raymond. As he opened the cafe door a shower of sunlight washed over the tables. Raymond closed his eyes against the brightness. When he opened them, Ernest had gone.

Raymond was unsure what to do. He still had coffee left, but it felt uncomfortable sitting in The Salt Shaker alone with the owner.

'You won't find a nicer gentleman than Ernest,' said Keith as he strode over to collect the cups. 'And gentleman is absolutely the right word. Ernest says everything happens for a reason, and maybe it does, but I think you have to take a few chances in life to make things happen, don't you? I wouldn't be here in The Shaker if I hadn't taken a risk or two.'

Raymond nodded and pushed back his chair, his mind made up.

He offered Keith a timid thank-you and hurried out of the cafe. The bell on the door jangled behind him as he set off in pursuit of Ernest.

CHAPTER SIX

The Biggest Smile

Raymond rushed down the road and caught up with the old man just as he was about to get into a dark-blue Morris Minor. The car was pristine; even its black tyres were devoid of dirt.

From a distance Ernest had seemed sad and preoccupied, as if the weight of the world were on his old shoulders, but on seeing Raymond a smile bloomed on his lips and his eyes twinkled back the years. He moved quickly around the car and vigorously shook Raymond's hand, then guided him into the passenger seat, his palm resting on Raymond's back.

The two men travelled in silence, but Ernest's smile remained in place the whole way. They drove out of town, around the confusing new roundabouts that resembled the Olympic rings, then followed the bus route along the New London Road. Raymond watched the familiar streets and landmarks of his bus journey pass by and thought about how his panic would usually increase the closer he got to home.

He was unsure what to do or what to say and the silence overwhelmed him as it had in the cafe. Powerless to stop the heat rising to his cheeks once more, he focused his gaze out of the side window, feigning interest in the scenery until his neck ached with the effort.

Every now and again Ernest would glance over. If he noticed Raymond's discomfort he made no mention of it.

At last they turned into Raymond's road.

'Okay, it's just over here on the left. Just drop me anywhere. Yes, this will do. Thank you very much for the lift.'

'My pleasure,' said Ernest. 'Are those sunflowers?' he asked, looking past Raymond into the garden.

'Er, yes. I'm trying to grow them but they're not doing very well.'

'I love sunflowers; they're my favourites. I have lots in my garden. Can I see them?'

Ernest stopped the car outside the small semi and got out. He looked at the untidy lawn. White daisies covered most of the front garden. A small brick wall marked its boundary and there were bedding plants flowering in the narrow borders. Raymond's sunflowers stood pallid against the light-red brick of the house.

'Can I have a closer look?' Ernest asked again. He stood on the driver's side of the car, his arms resting on the roof as he gazed over at the garden.

'Yes, okay. If you want to.'

Raymond held the small metal gate open and Ernest

strolled through. He walked slowly over the lawn, then stopped and turned, taking in the whole of the garden. The borders, though well stocked with bedding plants and mature shrubs, were a little unkempt and weedy but Raymond's patch was immaculate. Ernest smiled as they neared the sunflowers.

They knelt in front of the green stems and Ernest reached out to inspect a leaf.

'Did you know that sunflowers were around four thousand years ago?' he said. 'They used to be grown by American Indians. They'd grind the seed into flour for bread and use the oil on their skin and hair.' Ernest pulled off a curled brown leaf and let it drop to the grass. 'And in Peru, the Aztecs used them to crown their priestesses.' He straightened, wincing at the effort. 'Can you imagine? As far as the eye can see, rows and rows of sunflowers. What a sight that must have been.'

Raymond tilted his head slightly and looked at Ernest, intrigued.

'You know a lot about sunflowers?' he said.

'Well, a little.'

'In my book it says they can grow six feet in five months. That's fourteen inches a month, so that should be at least three inches a week.' The words burst from Raymond without pause or breath. 'But mine grow nowhere near that much. It's been nearly three months since I planted them, so I reckon they should be at least three and a half feet, but look at them – they're barely two.' Raymond glanced at Ernest, now embarrassed by his display of enthusiasm.

Ernest smiled. 'Ahhh,' he said quietly, 'so there *is*

something that gives you a spark, that makes you smile, that makes the day worth getting up for.' He turned and looked at Raymond. 'What are these flowers called, young man?'

'Sunflowers,' Raymond said, looking at the grass.

'That's right, sunflowers. Look at yours; they're in the shade. They love the sun. They want to bathe in its rays, hold their heads towards it, worship it.' It was Ernest's turn to become animated; he turned his weathered face to the sky and held out his arms.

'Well, my book says they don't mind some shade,' said Raymond, feeling a little defensive.

'Yes, some shade, but yours are in perpetual darkness.' Ernest began to laugh.

'But it's out of the wind here,' said Raymond. 'They'll get blown over if I move them. And if I put them near the road, someone will probably knock them down. In the shade they're safe.'

'I know, but they'll never get the chance to bloom. Surely that's not right. It's got to be worth the risk to see those wonderful flowers. Raymond, we have to give them a chance. Your sunflowers are cold. Let me come round tomorrow and I'll help you move them.'

Raymond turned towards Ernest in surprise.

'Well … what? I don't know … I don't know what we're doing tomorrow. I'll have to ask my mum.'

Ernest straightened his back slowly but it was clear he was excited.

'I'm not doing anything else. It would be wonderful! We can get to know each other. We already have something in common. I don't get out much. Could I help?' Ernest was talking so fast it shocked Raymond when he ran out of words and a silence ensued.

Raymond shook his head, pondering the situation. He looked up at Ernest.

'Well … okay, then. I suppose it'll be all right.'

'You know, Raymond, if all the smiles in all the world could be melted into one and if each of us could choose a moment to wear that smile, I would choose this one.'

* * *

Raymond lay in bed with the covers pulled high over his shoulders. A night light turned the darkness to a warm red that made the room feel safe and cosy. The sunflower book with its ruffled pages and bent corners lay discarded on the floor. Raymond pushed his hands together in prayer, his eyes shut tightly. He whispered the usual litany and each time he finished a prayer he crossed the opposing fingers of each hand to allow him to keep track of how many he'd said.

'Amen. Nineteen.' He crossed his ring fingers so only the little ones now remained upright. 'Gentle Jesus, meek and mild, look upon a little child. Pity my simplicity. Suffer me to come to thee. God bless Mum, Dad, nannies, granddads, aunties, uncles, cousins John and Clive, and all kind friends, and make Ray a good boy, for Jesus' sake. And thank you, Lord and everyone, for making the bus trip okay. Can you please make my giro come tomorrow? Thirty prayers if it comes tomorrow, promise. Amen. Twenty.' He flattened his little fingers.

Raymond sat up. He turned his top pillow over so he would feel the coolness of the other side when he went to sleep, then adjusted his blankets and settled back down. He lay bathed in the red haze for several minutes. He felt content and happily mulled over the day's events.

A notion took flight and he spun on to his right side so that his heart was again facing towards heaven. He closed his eyes, pushed his hands together and whispered into them, 'And, Lord, thank you so much for making me meet Ernest.'

CHAPTER SEVEN

The Lost Giro (Part Two)

The next morning, Raymond sat at the breakfast table eating his cornflakes. The sunflower book was propped against the marmalade jar, its pages wedged open by a salt-and-pepper pot.

'Raymond, what have I told you about reading at the table?' his mother said.

'Sorry, Mum. I'm just at an important bit.'

Raymond looked up from his cereal. His mum wore a crisp, recently washed, yellow-and-white chequered apron. She was busy drying the plates with a matching tea towel. There was a constant clatter as she placed the crockery in the cupboard.

'Okay but don't do it in front of your dad.'

'Thanks, Mum,' Raymond said, but he still felt the injustice of his dad being allowed to read the newspaper at the kitchen table every day.

The post fell through the letter box with a rattle and

a clunk. Raymond's mum put her tea towel down and went to collect it. He could hear her sorting through the envelopes.

'Whatever you said, it worked; your giro's here,' she called from the hallway.

Raymond could hardly believe it and tried not to smile as he spooned cornflakes into his mouth.

'Yes, I told them, Mum,' he shouted triumphantly between mouthfuls. 'I said it had to come today or they'd need to replace it. They said they'd send it straight away.'

'Well done, Ray. I'm so proud of you. And Dad will be pleased when he gets home from work.'

His mum returned to the kitchen and passed him the official-looking brown envelope with the letters DHSS written along the top.

'Open it, Ray. Maybe they've given you a bit extra for all the inconvenience.'

Raymond opened the envelope, took out the papers and unfolded them. He read the top one before rifling through the remaining paperwork. There was no giro.

'It says my money's going up; they must have forgotten to put the giro in.' He kept his eyes on the envelope, purposely avoiding his mother's gaze.

'Oh, Ray, what are they doing?' His mum slammed the other post on to the kitchen table with such uncharacteristic force that it made Raymond jump. 'You need to go straight back down there. Jessie next door had hers over the counter. You have to make a nuisance of yourself, Ray. Put your foot down.' She untied her apron. 'Look, I'll come with you; we'll see them together.'

'No, Mum. And, anyway, I can't go this morning – my friend's coming round.'

Raymond's mum stopped what she was doing. She looked at him, then to the letters, and then back. The double take seemed almost comical.

'Your friend?' she said. 'What friend, Ray?'

'Oh, I met him yesterday at the social,' Raymond replied casually. 'He seems nice.'

'Well … well, I'm really pleased. That's lovely. I'm going into town soon but perhaps I'll meet him when I get back.'

'He's only staying a little while, Mum,' he said quickly. 'Just to help me move my flowers.'

'Your sunflowers? Does he like gardening, then?'

'Yes, he really likes it. He's got sunflowers himself.'

He watched his mother look about her, as if trying to think of something to do. She seemed at a loss for words.

'Well, that's so nice, darling. I'm just a little surprised; most boys your age seem to like football and things like that. Anyway, you have a lovely morning. I'll see you later. Don't forget to make him a cup of tea or something, and there's biscuits in the tin.'

Raymond stayed at the kitchen table, listening to his mum in the hallway as she put on her coat and shoes. She called a goodbye and the front door clunked behind her.

He felt a little guilty; he'd not lied but he'd not been entirely truthful either. He knew that he should have mentioned Ernest's age, but was sure his mum would disapprove and he didn't want to lose this feeling of warm anticipation. He ran up the stairs to his bedroom, pulled on his gardening jeans and picked up the sunflower book. It wasn't long before he was bounding over the garden towards the shade, ready to rescue his straggly flowers.

CHAPTER EIGHT

A Risky Move

It was a bright sunny morning. Raymond and Ernest worked busily in the garden. Scattered over the lawn were trowels, clippers, spades and various other gardening paraphernalia.

Ernest bent over the flowers and dug carefully around their roots while Raymond watched intently, holding the stem upright as Ernest worked. Two large half-finished glasses of orange cordial stood beside them.

'We're risking it,' said Ernest. 'I was thinking last night, it's the wrong time to move them; it should have been sooner. We've got to make sure we get the roots up in one ball. Then they might stand a chance. You'll have to keep an eye on them, you know. Regular watering.'

'I know,' said Raymond quietly. 'I've plenty of time.'

'I was wondering about that.' Ernest paused and wiped his brow. 'Raymond, what do you like to do with your time?'

'I don't know. Nothing really. I like reading … my flowers. My dad wants me to find a job in London, but I don't know what to do.'

Ernest stood up and looked down at Raymond.

'You know, Raymond, you can do whatever you want, but you have to want to do it enough – more than anything else.'

'That's the trouble, I don't know what I want to do.' Raymond raised his head. He felt sad. 'Sometimes I want to stay in my room, draw the curtains and let the day pass me by.'

'Oh, I'm sorry to hear that.' Ernest offered his hand and pulled Raymond up. 'There are so many beautiful things in the world. Look, have you ever truly studied a flower?'

Ernest guided him to the border and knelt beside a small Busy Lizzie. Raymond followed the older man's lead and knelt too.

'Now, look at this flower closely; at the petals – the way they overlap, the way light shimmers on them. Look at the colours, Raymond. They're not one colour are they but many, each changing and blending into the next.'

Raymond placed his hands on the grass and bent forward so his face was inches from the flower. The petals appeared translucent as the sun shimmered through them, fizzing and illuminating the golden flecks of pollen. The colours were so vibrant that they seemed to pulse with life. Raymond sat back on his haunches.

'That's so beautiful,' he said, shaking his head in amazement. Despite his love of flowers, he'd always looked at them as a collection of colour rather than reaching deeper for their individuality.

Ernest smiled. 'Yes, and there's so much more you'll miss if you're stuck in your room. We need to get you out, Raymond.' Ernest dug around the sunflowers. 'We could spend some time together this summer; I've nothing particular to do. I could show you the places that are special to me and we could visit some of your favourites too.'

'I don't know … I don't really go anywhere,' Raymond said.

'What about when you were little?'

Raymond shook his head and shrugged. 'I don't know. I like the seaside.' He stood up. 'My mum and me would sit on the beach and dad would always go off exploring and bring back ice creams when he'd finished. We'd build sandcastles and tunnels and wait for the water to fill the moat and …'

The memory lay deep inside – those happy days at the beach, often spent with his cousins. The sun, the blue sky, the cooling breeze. Such excitement and a little trepidation when they boarded the train. It separated at Thorpe-le-Soken, about half way to their destination – the first four coaches heading for Clacton, the last four for Walton. A strange silence would befall their carriage as the shudder, clunk and metallic screech of the uncoupling took place. The boys would hold their breath and look wide-eyed at their parents until they felt the slow, staccato pull of the engine and their journey resumed.

The two families filled a single compartment. Buckets, spades, flasks and sandwiches, wrapped in greaseproof paper – all in over-stretched plastic carrier bags positioned haphazardly over the seats. The boys' laughter as they called to passers-by from the open window, then dived to the floor when they turned to look, was shrill and deafening until the adults quietened the excitement, only for it to build, and build again.

Raymond stared into space and smiled.

'Wakey-wakey,' said Ernest kindly. 'We'll go to the seaside then. I haven't been there for ages.'

'I'll have to ask my mum … I-I'm not sure.'

'Okay, have a think about it. Come on. Let's move these flowers.'

The two men worked in silence, concentrating on their efforts, each falling naturally into their respective roles. Raymond bowed to Ernest's greater experience, the junior surgeon attending a major operation, supplying the tools and an extra pair of hands. Ernest dug expertly around the base of each flower, patient and gentle, never forcing the plant from the soil until the roots were free.

A couple of hours later, the men stood back to admire their work. They had transferred the line of sunflowers from the shaded side of the house to a border by the front wall of the garden. Each plant now stood straight and tall, anchored to a bamboo cane firmly embedded in the soil. The sun shone brightly overhead, and as it moved across the sky towards the house, the sunflowers cast shadows on the road that seemed to breathe with the breeze. A bold dark wave on the cold, hard concrete.

'There, finished,' said Ernest happily. 'It's been a wonderful morning. Thank you for letting me help.' He stamped his feet, dislodging some of the mud from his shoes. 'Water them every day and keep your fingers crossed.' He reached into his pocket and pulled out a small piece of paper and a pen. 'Look, this is my address and phone number. If you want to meet again give me a call.' Ernest wrote his details on the paper.

'Would you like another drink before you go?' asked Raymond shyly. 'I could show you my sunflower book.'

'Well, that would be lovely. I am very thirsty.'

Raymond opened the front door. They took off their dirty shoes and padded through the hallway into the kitchen. Raymond poured two large glasses of orange squash and they sat down at the kitchen table.

'Ah, just what the doctor ordered,' said Ernest, stretching.

'Did he?' said Raymond, puzzled. 'Are you … are you okay? Um, I'll just get my book.'

* * *

Ernest smiled as Raymond pushed his chair back and hurriedly ran for the stairs. He leant forward on to the kitchen table, trying to relieve some of the pressure on his aching back. Sitting down had made him realise just how tired he was. His legs and arms felt stiff and heavy. He hated the way old age had crept up on him, and his unforgiving joints annoyed him. It had been a long time since he'd done that much manual work; his own garden more or less took care of itself.

Fight it. Fight it.

He took another sip of his squash and looked around the kitchen. The tiling, although not to his taste, made it so much easier to clean. He made a mental note to do the same in his own kitchen when it needed redecoration.

Ernest heard the front door open. Then a fumbling of bags and keys before it slammed shut. A woman's voice called from the hallway.

'Ray, are you home? The sunflowers look lovely there. You have been busy.'

Ernest half-stood. Unsure what to do next; he remained in a crouch, facing the unopened kitchen door.

'Yes, Mum. Thanks. My friend's—'

The kitchen door opened. Raymond's mother screamed and lifted a can of baked beans.

'I am terribly sorry to have startled you,' said Ernest, who had retreated to the kitchen sink and was keeping the large table between them. His hands were raised in supplication.

'I'm Ernest Gardiner. I've been helping your son with his sunflowers.' He lowered his right hand and held it out to Raymond's mum in the hope she would shake it. She ignored his hand and Ernest tried to disguise the attempt by scratching his other arm.

'Oh! You frightened me,' she said, brushing imaginary fluff from her coat.

Raymond stumbled into the kitchen, barely catching his breath.

'Hello, Mum. Er, this is the friend I was telling you about.'

His mother concentrated on her shopping, lifting the heavy bags awkwardly on to the kitchen table. She looked at the tin of beans, as if surprised it was still in her hand,

and quickly placed it inside the cupboard with the others.

Then she looked at Ernest.

'Pleased to meet you.' Her tone was polite but Ernest could see accusation and fury in her eyes. He looked away quickly.

'This is the book I was telling you about,' said Raymond.

Ernest, half-heartedly flicked through the pages, his gaze constantly wrenched towards Raymond's mum, who could barely disguise her rage.

'This is lovely, Raymond,' he said, glancing across the kitchen, 'but I really must be going. Thanks for the drink. If you'd like to meet up sometime, don't forget I've put my details on this piece of paper here. It was nice to meet you, Mrs Mann.'

He eased sideways past Raymond's mum and nodded. An icy stare met his convivial smile, and he quickly returned his gaze to the floor. Raymond followed him out of the kitchen and opened the front door.

'Thank you so much for helping me today,' said Raymond. 'I could never have done it without you.' The words flew from his smiling mouth.

* * *

Though he realised he'd upset his mum, and that Ernest was making a hasty escape, Raymond desperately wanted to make things right. He couldn't lose this new, unlikely friend. He sought the courage to reach out and shake Ernest's hand but felt awkward and didn't know how to make that happen.

'The sunflowers look fantastic. They're all straight and … and, well, I'll talk to mum about the trip to the seaside. I'd really like to go.'

Ernest smiled. 'I'd like that as well. Fingers crossed, then.'

Raymond watched as Ernest walked down the path and out of the gate. His new friend passed the front wall and stopped to look at the sunflowers, still bathed in dazzling yellow light. Raymond raised a hand to shield his eyes from the sun. As the shadow fell across them, easing his view, he saw Ernest, partly obscured by the green leaves, jumping excitedly up and down, his arms high in triumph, fists clenched as if he'd just scored a goal for England. Then he waved and continued along the pavement to his car, doing another little jump and skip when he reached it.

Raymond laughed and returned the wave, astounded that anyone, especially a grown-up, could act in such a way.

He walked back into the kitchen, smiling and humming a song to himself. He'd not felt this happy for an age. His mum was putting away the remaining shopping but she turned quickly, still holding a couple of cereal boxes.

'What on earth were you thinking, letting an old man like that into the house? You have no idea what he might have done. You've got to be so careful these days.'

Her words stung, harsh and cold, slapping him out of his revelry.

'What do you mean? He's … he's really nice. He helped me at the social and he moved all my sunflowers.'

'Raymond, you don't understand; you don't even know him. Why on earth would an old man like that want to be friends?'

Raymond felt the familiar heat rise to his cheeks. 'This morning, you were pleased when I said I *had* a friend.'

'Yes, but that was before I found out he was a *hundred years old.*'

Raymond paused deciding on another approach. He spoke quietly, in the hope his mother would have a change of heart.

'Mum, he's nice. He helped me. You can't put an age on a friendship, can you?' He looked down at the floor. 'And, anyway, he's invited me round to his house.'

'*What?* Well you're not going. It's just not right; it's not natural. You're definitely not going, Raymond, and that's that. I'm not arguing—'

'But, Mum!' His voice was a squeak but he carried on regardless, despite his embarrassment. 'You can't stop me! I want to. He's really interesting. He listens to me, asks me what I want to do. He knows about sunflowers and everything.'

'We'd listen to you, Ray, if only you'd talk to us.' His mum spoke slowly, emphasising each word. 'But you're always in your room.' She shook her head. 'Let's see what your dad says. Why you can't find friends of your own age, I don't know. You haven't spoken to anyone since you left school, have you? And you didn't even go to the reunion.'

The words tore into Raymond and he recoiled from the rancid memories that flashed through his head. The reunion had been a big event, organised one year after everyone had left school. Raymond's old friends had either been invited or had heard about the plans through word of mouth. No one had thought to tell him. Sometime later, his friends had been talking about the party and Raymond discovered he had missed it. Although his friends all apologised, each saying they'd assumed one of the others had told him, Raymond had felt hurt for weeks afterwards. The nagging suspicion that they hadn't wanted him there in the first place, left him feeling insecure and sad.

'That's because no one invited me or even told me about it!' he said, his voice shrill and loud. He stormed out of the kitchen and up the stairs.

His mum called after him. 'I know, Ray. I'm sorry – that was horrible of them, but sometimes *you* need to make an effort though. I … I just want you to be—'

Raymond turned. 'Normal, you just want me to be normal.'

He slammed the bedroom door behind him.

'Happy,' she said gently. 'I just want you to be happy.'

CHAPTER NINE

Ernest's House

The packed bus didn't help Raymond's state of agitation.

There were three stops to go before his and he watched in horror as the conductor pursued several new passengers up the stairs. He felt the familiar tension in his chest as each breath failed to fill his lungs.

'Oh, no. Please no,' he muttered. 'Lord, ten prayers tonight if you make her come back down before my stop.'

The chances of her returning to the lower deck before the bus reached his destination were slim. He looked about to see if there was any other movement in the passengers around him.

An old lady stood, rang the bell and hobbled towards the exit. The engine slowed and, without thinking, Raymond jumped to his feet and followed her off the bus.

Hot, sweaty and still shaking, he rested his hands on his knees and took a deep, cooling breath of fresh air. He looked at his watch. Although he'd alighted two stops too soon, he could still be on time. Smiling, he began to half-run, half-skip towards his destination.

* * *

Raymond looked down at the creased slip of paper. Spindly blue writing formed an address. Forty-three. This was it. He walked cautiously up the gravel drive, his footsteps scrunching on the stones despite his efforts to move quietly.

He was breathing hard; it had taken him longer than expected and this, together with a feeling of reckless excitement, made his heartbeat quicken.

The house was old-fashioned but well looked after, probably built at the turn of the century. It seemed sturdy and substantial compared to Raymond's new-build estate home. White gloss shone on the newly painted window frames.

The garden was immaculate. Borders overflowed with shrubs and flowers, each complementing the other in size, shape and colour – a testament to the time lovingly spent on the design. By the wall, bathed in sunlight, were a dozen large sunflowers already in bloom. Raymond stood spellbound, feeling himself drawn across the finely cut lawn for a closer look.

He stared upwards in admiration.

Each flower was at least six feet tall. The large yellow heads nodded heavily, petals tickled by the breeze, the colour accentuated by the bright sunlight. Raymond gently brushed his hand over a rich green leaf and felt its fine nap hold his fingers like a cat's tongue.

'Hello.'

Raymond jumped, quickly retracting his hand. He turned and, seeing Ernest, began to laugh.

'You made me jump.'

Ernest smiled. 'I'm sorry. I seem to have that effect on your family.' They stood side by side, looking at the sunflowers. 'Thanks for coming; I didn't think you would somehow. I know your mum didn't like me much, and why should she? An old fellow like me, friends with her son? I can see her point … why are you so out of breath?'

Raymond returned his gaze to the sunflowers. He felt once more transfixed and replied absent-mindedly, 'It's a long story. I … I don't like getting off buses. These are amazing. Why are they in bloom when mine have barely a bud? And, er, my mum doesn't know I'm here. She wants me to have friends but when I find one, she doesn't like it.'

Ernest shook his head but continued to smile.

'They're in bloom because they've found where they belong. They're round pegs in round holes, not square ones like yours.'

Raymond frowned and mouthed, *Round pegs in round holes?*

Ernest laughed. 'Where have you been all your life, Raymond? You aren't very good at sayings, are you? And don't blame your mother; all she does, she does because she loves you and wants you to be happy and safe. I can still remember the last time my own mother held me tightly all those years ago. I could smell her flowery scent, hear her heart quicken, and I knew all she wanted to do was keep me safe from the war. She must have felt my grip tighten, because she squeezed me once more, then gently moved away while still holding my hands. She leant forward and kissed my cheek and said, "Time to fly, son." I've never forgotten it and I never held my mother like that again. I can still remember it like yesterday. When you get home, give your mum a big hug. One of these days it will be your turn to fly and those hugs will never be quite the same again.'

Raymond shuddered. 'Oh no, I couldn't,' he said, shaking his head and taking a step backwards. 'I don't hug anyone. It just feels weird.'

Ernest laughed. 'You don't know what you're missing. Come on – let's get a cup of tea and we can talk about the summer.'

Ernest opened the front door and Raymond followed him inside to the hallway of a tidy and nicely decorated home. It didn't have the sharp lines of his parents' house and Raymond felt at ease as soon as he entered.

Ornaments covered most of the flat surfaces and on a high wooden shelf multiple knick-knacks immortalising special memories were displayed.

By the front door on a thin wooden table, Raymond noticed a single black-and-white photograph surrounded by a silver frame. It showed a beautiful young woman, her dark hair tied back. She was laughing.

They moved into the lounge and Ernest led Raymond to a comfortable-looking armchair with several plumped cushions.

'Make yourself at home,' he said. 'There are gardening books over there. I think there's one on sunflowers if you can find it. Tea or coffee?' Ernest disappeared into the kitchen as he spoke.

'Oh, tea, please. Could I have two sugars?'

Raymond reached across and flicked through a magazine rack next to the armchair, then stood, stretched and walked over to a bookcase stuffed with publications of every sort. He pulled out one or two books and browsed the pages, but both failed to hold his attention and he replaced them and wandered around the room.

Through the large patio doors, he could see a beautifully kept back garden. Shrubs and trees moved in the gentle breeze. For once, he didn't linger on the flowers but, instead, turned to explore the room. His gaze was drawn to a sepia photograph in a dark-brown frame on the far wall. It showed several horses with riders leading a group of men. Raymond moved closer to study the picture. The men were soldiers. Behind them, the sun shimmered through the morning mist and bounced off silver puddles. All around was thick dark mud and a forest of broken trees.

Ernest returned to the lounge holding a tray with tea and biscuits on it.

'Ah, I see you've found my photographs. A long time ago I used to be a photographer; it was my job. I loved it. Would you like to see some of my other pictures?' He put the tray down on a small coffee table, walked over to a large wooden cabinet and opened a drawer.

'A photographer?' Raymond couldn't conceal his excitement. 'Yes, please. I'd like that.' He picked up his teacup.

Ernest pulled out a large photograph album and handed

it over. Raymond turned the pages slowly, revealing faded black-and-white photographs protected by yellowing plastic. Beneath each picture was a name, written in Ernest's spidery blue handwriting: Gene Tierney, Rita Hayworth, Jennifer Jones, Joseph Cotton, James Stewart, Orson Welles. Raymond turned another page, this one seemed devoted to large orchestras: The Berlin Philharmonic, The New York Symphony, The Vienna Philharmonic.

'I seemed to be the go-to person for classical albums years ago,' said Ernest with more than a hint of pride in his voice. 'You can still buy those records with my photographs on their covers today.'

'But ... but you're famous,' said Raymond. 'Even I know some of these people and album covers. That's fantastic.' He looked again at the far wall. 'What about that one?' he said, pointing to the sepia picture. 'That one must be special.'

'Well, that was where my career started. I was a photographer in the First World War. Do you know much about what we call The Great War?'

'Yes, we learnt about it at school. First World War poetry. I really liked it.'

'I can tell you, Raymond, there was nothing to like about that war. It was terrible and it changed my life. Of all the pictures I took, I can only look at this one.' Ernest moved closer to the photograph. 'There just seems to be some hope in it; the sun is still shining and the forest is still growing. Look there ...' Ernest pointed to the bottom corner of the photograph. 'You can just see the tiny shoots picking their way through the mud.'

'Oh, yes … yes, I can see them!' said Raymond, squinting.

'It was a dreadful time, but at the end of the war I met my wife and I began my life again.' He smiled. 'Everything happens for a reason.'

'Your wife? You're married? I didn't know.'

'Yes, for fifty years. She died three years ago and not a day goes by without me thinking about her. We had the happiest of times. Have you ever been in love, Raymond?'

'No,' said Raymond, uninvited warmth invading his cheeks.

'Oh, you will,' said Ernest, smiling. 'And it's the greatest feeling in the world. You'll buy each other gifts, have pet names for each other, you might even have your own language.' He laughed. 'Does liccle-iccle Waymond want his tea?'

'I will *never* do that,' said Raymond, horrified. 'I'm sure my mum and dad don't.'

'Mark my words, you will. And I bet they did before you came along.'

'What was your wife's name,' said Raymond, determined to change the conversation.

Ernest pointed to another photograph in which he stood beside a portly but elegant woman with tightly curled white hair and a smile so gentle that Raymond felt as if his heart were being brushed by snow.

'Violet.'

Raymond studied the photograph. 'She looks beautiful and … and kind.'

'You have a way with words. Thank you. And you're

right, she was beautiful and kind, and I don't think you can have a better combination than that, do you?'

Raymond continued to scrutinise the picture. 'She looks different to the lady in the photograph by the front door though; it's not the same person, is it?' he said.

'Ah, that's a picture of Mira. She was French and I met her during the war. I have only been in love twice in my life; once for a few weeks and once for over fifty years. Mira was my first love.'

'Really? What happened?' said Raymond, intrigued.

'Oh, Raymond! We're here to talk about the summer – the future – not what happened in my past.'

'But it's interesting. Tell me more,' implored Raymond.

'I'll tell you what, you come up with five things to do this summer and I'll tell you the story.'

'Okay. Well, I like the seaside,' said Raymond quickly.

Ernest laughed. 'That's a start, but you've already mentioned that one.'

There was a long pause. Raymond stared into space, thinking intently, his mouth moving slightly.

'There must be other things,' said Ernest after a while.

'There are, I know there are. I just can't think of anything right now. Er, gardening?' he said, wondering if that counted.

'Great, we'll go to Kew Gardens. It's fantastic there – so many plants from all around the world. There's one called the corpse flower that smells awful and only blooms once in a blue moon. Maybe we'll be lucky and see it.'

'I'll have a think. It's not just me though – we have to do things you want to do too,' said Raymond.

'We will. Okay, I'll have a think as well. Anyway, you've heard a bit about me and my photography; tell me about you. What do you want to do with your life?'

'You sound like my dad. I-I don't know.' A sense of hopelessness overwhelmed Raymond momentarily.

'Well, what do you like? What inspires you?' Ernest said, his clenched hand pumping with each word.

'I don't know, gardening I suppose … umm, I liked those First World War poems. They made me think. There was one by William Owen – it had a long name.'

'Wilfred Owen,' said Ernest, 'and you're probably thinking of "Dulce et Decorum Est".'

'Yes, yes, that was it,' Raymond said excitedly as he put down his cup.

'That's a wonderful poem, one of my favourites. So you like words?'

'Er, yes, I suppose I do,' said Raymond.

Ernest smiled. 'Well, you should try to write them down. I enjoyed photography so much it didn't seem like a job; it was just fun. You can be a writer or a gardener, anything. Find something you enjoy though.' He leant back in his armchair and chuckled. 'Oh, I wish I could have your years again, Raymond. The things I'd do, especially now that I'm not worried about what people think of me.'

Raymond's anxiety began to take hold; he really had no idea what to do with his life. On many a cold, dark evening he'd sat in his room, thinking hard about the future but unable to picture himself achieving anything. When he was little and his friends had wanted to drive tractors or trains, or be footballers or doctors, nothing had ever appealed. Was there something lacking in him? If there were, he didn't want Ernest to know. He looked at his watch, exaggerating the movement, then stood.

'I know, I will write them down. That's a really good idea. Actually it took longer to get here than I thought and I've just remembered I've got to do something for my mum. I'm going to have to go. I'm really sorry.'

Ernest rose quickly from his chair. He raised his hands, the palms facing outwards.

'Goodness, I'm so sorry. Who am I to tell you about life? Especially you with your whole future ahead of you. You'll make mistakes, we all do, but it's allowed. I reckon that if you're kind, have a dream or two and try not to say *What if* too many times, it will all be fine. I promise it will.'

He reached across and touched Raymond's arm, but Raymond instinctively pulled away.

'Don't go just yet,' Ernest said gently. 'Let me tell you about Mira, or should I say Mirabelle. That name means "wonderful" or "incredible beauty", and both those definitions suit her perfectly.'

'Well, er, I don't know,' said Raymond. 'I ... I still can't be late.'

'Let's just see how we get on then, shall we? You go when you need to.'

Raymond sat back down in the armchair. 'Okay,' he said, trying not to smile.

Ernest sighed, as if relieved, and settled back into his chair, linking his fingers over his stomach.

'Right, where do I start,' he said.

CHAPTER TEN

Ernest's Story (Part One)

1917

A column of soldiers moved towards the brow of a hill. Ahead of them a small group of riders mounted on large brown horses led the way. Panniers slung on either side of the horses weighed them down, and as they trudged through the mud, they held their heads low.

The mood of the khaki-clad men seemed upbeat and cheerful in contrast. It was a spring day and a shimmering mist shrouded the pathway. Shards of silver sunlight broke through the trees and bounced off puddles, dazzling the men as they marched forwards.

At the top of the hill a photographer stood by the side of the road. He steadied a large, square camera on his chest and looked downwards through the viewfinder as the troop trudged past.

'Hey, Ernie, make sure you get my best side,' one of the soldiers shouted.

'You haven't got a best side, Bill,' said Ernest, laughing.

'How about this then?' Bill pretended to undo his trousers and show his bottom to the camera. The men laughed and swaggered.

At the front of the column, an officer turned his horse and shouted, 'Fall in. Quiet back there.'

The men quickly got back in line, grumbling. As they marched past Ernest, he took his photograph.

Through the morning mist, Bill looked back at Ernest, smiled and stuck his middle finger up. Ernest returned the gesture.

* * *

The men sat in a line, keenly drawing on their tiny roll-ups. There was low laughter and chatter in the air, but they looked pale and drawn. Light-brown mud daubed their uniforms. Their bench was built of slats of wood and a large, mud-clad trench piled high with sandbags, provided their shelter. Distant gunfire rumbled, then came the thud of an explosion. One soldier crouched on the fire-step – a ledge cut three feet higher than the wooden planking of the trench floor – and looked out over no man's land.

Ernest was young and looked fragile, his dark hair fashionably swept back and longer than most of his comrades'. The years had not yet broadened his body.

Next to him sat Bill – hardy, weather-beaten, his skin lined and tanned, hair cut short. Dark stubble prickled his face. He wore his sleeves rolled up and the muscles in his forearms moved visibly as he prepared a small cigarette.

Despite the many months of hardship, he still looked strong and fit. He passed the finished roll-up to Ernest.

'So, you jammy sod, how'd you get to take photographs while we're all running round like headless chickens?'

'Oh, it's a long story,' said Ernest. 'A bloke called Ernest Brooks saw my Kodak.' He lifted a black oblong case tied around his neck. 'He asked if I knew how to use it, and when I said I loved taking pictures, he told me the army needed official photographers. The next day he gave me this.' Ernest hoisted a much larger black box from the duckboards beneath his feet and placed it heavily on his lap. He moved a lever and the box concertinaed open to reveal a camera lens and viewfinder. 'It's called a Goerz-Anschütz and, would you believe it, it's bloody German. It needs to be big to take photographs good enough for the newspapers, but I have to carry round these glass plates as well and they weigh a ton, so it's not all glamour.'

'At least you haven't had to go to the front line,' said Bill.

'Until now,' said Ernest quietly. 'I know it was the luckiest thing that ever happened to me, getting this' – he patted the camera – 'but now the papers want action.'

'You stick with me, mate. You'll be all right. This is my fourth campaign. There's only me left now from the Lyndhurst training.' Bill straightened his legs and stretched his arms. 'Everything happens for a reason. I'll be something after the war.'

'Be something what?' asked Ernest. 'I'm going straight back to my mother's house when this is all over.'

Bill laughed. 'Bloody hell, Ernie. Show some ambition mate. This war will give us ordinary blokes a chance. We can open a factory, become gamblers, marry a countess, anything you like. Believe me, there won't be enough chaps to go round. You know what I want?' Ernest shook his head. 'To open a place where people can be happy again, a theatre or restaurant. I don't know … something like that.'

A column of men trudged past and Bill quickly pulled in his legs. Ernest looked at their faces. Each had a dull, vacant expression, eyes focused on something far in the distance, oblivious to their surroundings. The chatter of the trench dropped sharply and a funereal silence fell.

'Poor sods,' said Bill once they were out of earshot. 'Front-line fodder.'

'God, we'll be there soon.' Ernest gave an involuntary shudder. 'Anyway, you don't know the first thing about theatres or restaurants, do you?'

'We'll invent the rules, mate. And you'll take photos of all the rich and famous people visiting Bill's brassiere.'

Ernest laughed. 'You mean brasserie – what you said means bra.'

'I think I was right first time, mate. It's bound to be full of tits.'

Both men looked at each other, then burst into unbridled laughter. Bill fell from his seat and knelt on the floor of the trench, his elbows on the bench and his head resting in his hands. His shoulders shook with each hooting convulsion.

A whistle blew.

'On your feet, lads!' a sergeant shouted as he walked down the line, pulling sleeping soldiers off the benches and kicking at outstretched legs. The moans and groans of the disturbed men filled the air with a dull drone. Ernest looked around at his companions and saw their eyes furtive with fear and resignation.

'Christ, they can't want us to go again,' hissed Bill. 'It's fucking madness; only a handful of us came back from the last one.'

Ernest shivered and felt the colour drain from his face, turning it into a pale glassy mask. Bill nudged him in the ribs playfully.

'Stick with me, Ernie. You'll be all right, mate.'

'I don't want to go,' whispered Ernest. 'I've taken hundreds of photos of dead people; I don't want to end up like that.'

The sergeant walked over and stopped in front of them. He was an older man, a powerful hardened soldier, his clipped moustache dark against his ruddy complexion.

'Well, what have we here?' he said, addressing the whole trench while looking down at Ernest. 'It's our official photographer joining us for once.' He turned to the men and raised his voice. 'Make sure you look good for the camera, boys!' The men laughed half-heartedly, their eyes lowered, not wishing to be the butt of the next joke. 'You're looking a shade pale, Gardiner. Everything all right?'

'He's fine, Sarge,' said Bill.

'Make sure he is. I've heard the papers are impatient for some pictures so I want you two at the front of the advance, in the thick of it. Right! Off your arses. Get your equipment on that pack horse, Gardiner. Double quick time. Let's go – everyone up.'

Dusk fell as the men moved through the maze of trenches that led to the front line. They walked for what seemed like hours but the sound of gunfire remained distant. Every few seconds an explosion lit the sky lightning like, allowing them to see the man ahead, hunched in resignation and terror, aware of his temporality.

There was a commotion at the head of the line.

'Move, move boys. Quick, let us through *now*.'

Desperate shouts and then the thud of boots on board. Wretched stretcher-bearers struggled to find their way through the reluctant muddle of men. Ernest looked down at their burden. A young man sprawled on the stretcher, head raised as if trying to direct the rescuers. His breath came in bloody gargles, the fine spray of red already colouring his uniform, but it was his stomach that drew Ernest's gaze. The soldier had lost most of the uniform covering his torso, exposing his ripped, bare flesh. Muscle and sinew shone in the strobing light and the man used his hands to hold his stomach closed and his bloody innards in place.

Ernest turned to the trench wall and vomited. He looked at Bill, his face white and drained.

'Come on, mate,' said Bill. 'It'll be okay. Stick with me.' Ernest felt himself half-pushed, half-dragged along the trench, his legs buckling with every step.

Smoke drifted across the winding column of men creating a ghostly haze. White ash stuck to their mud-encrusted uniforms and added to Ernest's fear that they were marching inexorably closer to a world of spirits.

The soldiers reached the final entrenchment and came

to a halt. Every few seconds yellow flares illuminated the night sky, then faded. Ernest surveyed his barren surroundings. Bombed and broken barbed-wire fences littered the landscape. Thick dark posts, snapped at odd angles, sprung from the ground, their earlier purpose now long forgotten.

A low, guttural cry invaded the silence. On the fire-step next to Ernest a sentry lowered his head and rested it in his open hand; his fingers clawed through his dark hair. He shook his head back and forth in hopeless surrender.

'Christ, make it stop. Please, God.' He turned to Ernest. 'He's been out there since this morning, trapped on the wire. He won't die.' The sentry gulped in the stagnant air and closed his eyes.

'Come over here, mate,' said Bill to Ernest, and dragged him down the line. He lit a cigarette, passed it to Ernest and squeezed his shoulder. Ernest took the cigarette gratefully but found his hands shook so violently he could not raise it to his lips. He tried three more times, but intensified trebling foiled each attempt. With a sigh, he clenched his fists and rested them by his side, the glowing roll-up still visible in the dark. Bill moved closer and guided the cigarette to Ernest's lips. Ernest closed his eyes, took a long slow drag, then released the smoke into the air, watching it swirl upwards towards the glistening stars.

They stood in silence for a while as the cigarettes smouldered.

'I don't want to move. I'm going to stay here,' Ernest said quietly.

'Come on, mate. You'll be okay; you're going to be someone, remember?'

Bill took the spent stub from Ernest's frozen fingers and threw it on to the trench floor. Then he rubbed Ernest's hands between his, warming them.

He smiled. 'You'll never be able to take any pictures like this, will you?'

* * *

The hours dragged by and the men remained huddled together, as much for comfort as for warmth. The first light of day seeped through the shadows and the sun's warming rays fell on their bloodless faces until whispered orders and silent shoves roused them from their slumber.

Ernest went to the packhorses to retrieve his camera, then joined the men standing three deep next to the trench wall – a line of dark khaki stretching as far as the eye could see. A few had hip flasks full of whisky and they passed these around to those lucky enough to be close by.

They waited for what seemed like hours, trying to avoid each other's gaze, afraid they'd witness their own mirrored terror.

A shrill peal shocked the silent line as their captain put his whistle to his lips and blew hard, a brain-wrenching scream of a signal. The men, eyes wide, veins bursting like racehorses', clambered over the trench wall and into the morning haze. The skies opened in a kaleidoscope of colour and light, as the soldier's desperate cries combined with the cacophony of gunfire and bomb blasts to make sounds that had never been made. Thuds moved kidneys and made heartbeats stutter as screams penetrated deep into the earth to a place below hell. Ahead of him soldiers disappeared into no man's land, led by their captain, who held a single revolver and waved his men forward like Ahab.

'I can't move.' Ernest knew the consequences of refusing to advance but accepted his fate. He shook his head. 'I can't go.'

'You have to, mate, or they'll shoot you here. Come on.'

Bill pulled Ernest upright and thrust him over the top of the trench.

Weighed down by the camera and canvas bag, he was like a rag doll. The strength left his legs and, jelly-like, he stumbled. Explosions spewed mud and debris in every direction. He tripped and staggered over the bloodied limbs of fallen comrades and he watched, helpless, as a stream of bullets zipped into those in front of him; they dropped instantly, their love, laughter, hopes and dreams gone in a heartbeat.

Twenty yards ahead, a deafening blast lofted Ernest and Bill into the air. They turned and spun before landing heavily on the soft ground.

* * *

Dazed and on all fours, Bill crawled through the mud in an ever-widening circle. He searched for his friend, oblivious to the zing of bullets and the eruptions that buckled his arms.

There was no sign of Ernest.

An explosion covered him in muddy debris. He lay on his stomach, his ears ringing; everything becoming a dull thud. He raised his head. Through the smoke, highlighted by a yellow flare, he saw a slight outline of a figure leap, then disappear.

Bill snaked forward through the mud. Gradually his hearing recovered and he was greeted once more by the nightmare of noise, the brief respite only intensifying the sensation. He neared his goal and found the path blocked by a huge shell hole. He turned slowly until his body was level with the lip, and rolled in.

Giddy and unsettled by the tumble, it took several minutes until he could breathe normally and for the nausea to pass. He looked up. At the far end of the hole was a small, frightened man with his back to the muddy wall. It was Ernest.

There was another explosion. Bill watched as Ernest fumbled on the ground, pulled his camera closer and wrapped his body around it. His mouth opened like a drowning fish and he screamed, silver spit glistened in the smoke. But there was no sound.

Ernest tried to stand, then dropped to his knees. Bill stumbled towards him, grasped his arm firmly and pulled him towards the other end of the shell hole.

'Ernest,' he whispered. There was no response; his friend's eyes were glazed and lifeless. 'Ernie,' he said again, louder now. Still no response. In desperation, he shouted as loud and as long as his lungs would last. 'Ernest, *get up*. NOW.'

Ernest turned his head and Bill saw the faintest spark of recognition in his eyes. He cradled his friend and, amid the outrageous roar, took Ernest's second box and smashed it on the wall until it rattled.

'Come on, mate. Let's get out of here!'

Ernest shook his head. 'What's the point? I can't keep going. Leave me here.'

'Can't do that. I told you, we're going to be something. There's a reason for us to get through this.'

Bill dragged Ernest up the side of the hole and into no man's land. Then, half-walking, half-sliding, the two men stumbled back through the clawing, sucking mud to their own line.

* * *

They slid down the side of their trench, covered in mud, breathing in deep joyful gulps of air, and collapsed on to the wooden duckboards. Ernest lay with his head propped on Bill's chest and through half-open eyes saw the sergeant approaching. He was angry; his cheeks were red, his eyes wide and bulging. As he neared them, he kicked out at odd bits of wood that had broken away from the trench wall. He stopped and stared at them for what seemed like an eternity.

'Well, well, what have we here? The heroes have returned.' His tone was bitter.

'We went right to their lines, Sarge. We couldn't have gone no further. Gardiner was a fucking hero. He was taking photos of the Hun's trench, then someone ordered the retreat – I think it was the captain.'

'Is that right, Gardiner?'

'Yes, sir,' Ernest mumbled.

'Well, I look forward to seeing the photographs, Gardiner. I'm sure they'll be just what the papers ordered.'

More battle-worn men returned to the trench, falling over the side and sliding into the mud and debris. They sat with their backs to the wall, their legs outstretched, hands holding lowered heads. Each gasp of air told them they were still alive, but that the nightmare was not yet over. Many nursed wounds, their uniforms a patchwork of deep-red. All looked bedraggled and traumatised.

Bill reached for Ernest's second bag.

'Here's all the glass plates, Sarge. Gardiner needs to get these developed.' As he raised the bag there was a jangling sound.

Bill opened the bag. 'Fuck, Sarge. Look.' He showed the sergeant hundreds of tiny broken pieces of glass and shook his head. 'Fucking hell, Sarge. All his work.'

Ernest stared at Bill and the bag. He felt his mouth opening in disbelief and made a conscious effort to close it.

A soldier ran towards them.

'Captain's dead, sir.'

The sergeant sighed, resigned and beaten. 'Oh God … thank you, Corporal.' He stared at Ernest and whispered, 'Poor bastard.' Then his voice rose. 'I'm watching you, son. I know there's something going on – not much gets past me. Next time, you stick with me, Gardiner. We'll get some special photos then.' The sergeant turned and marched quickly down the trench. He stopped and looked back at them. 'Sit here with the boys for a bit and then get back to town for some food.'

'Thank you, sir.' The two men spoke in unison, one much louder than the other.

* * *

They made their way in silence down the maze of trenches and came to the ruins of a once busy town. Ernest went to retrieve more glass plates for his camera while Bill got them bottles of cold beer. They found a straw-filled wagon and sat against a wheel in the bright sunlight. Slowly, the world returned to them.

'Thanks again, Bill. I was a goner,' said Ernest. 'I couldn't move.'

'Forget it mate. It's just one of those things. I've seen men go doolally at a lot less than that. You would've done the same for me.' Bill leaned forward and clunked his bottle against Ernest's. 'Anyway, don't talk about that. Come on; tell me what you're going to do after the war.'

'I don't know. Maybe take some more photos – I like doing that.' Ernest pulled the strap of his small Kodak over his head and laid it on his lap. He clicked the camera open, allowing the black bellows to expand, and looked through the viewfinder. 'Or I could just stick with you, mate. You seem to have all the answers.' He pointed the camera at Bill, who laughed.

'Put that away,' he said. 'And I don't have the answers. I just ask lots of questions. But, you know, I reckon everything happens for a reason and that's why we're mates.'

There was a commotion at the far end of the street. Ernest and Bill saw a soldier on horseback questioning a group of men. The men looked around, then pointed up the road in their direction. The rider saluted and reined his horse towards them.

'Private Gardiner? Is there a Private Gardiner?' he called out as he rode along the street.

'Over here, sir,' shouted Bill. 'Here he is. It's Ernie.'

The rider slowed his horse and looked down at them. 'Private Gardiner?'

'Um ... yes, sir.'

'Private Gardiner, the photographer?'

'He's the one sir,' said Bill. 'He's the best around.'

Ernest pointed to the camera lying next to him.

'Some bigwig up at HQ wants his war effort captured on film for the nation to enjoy,' said the rider in an upper-class British accent. 'You're the nearest blasted photographer. You need to get up there tout suite.'

Ernest looked at Bill, who shrugged.

'But where do I go? How do I get there?' he said.

'HQ's on the front line,' answered the horseman, 'but we haven't seen the bloody Hun for ages; you'll have a picnic up there. There's a transport leaving shortly – make sure you're on it.'

'But what about all my equipment? I can't move it by myself. It's far too much for one person.' Ernest glanced at Bill.

'I only have orders for you, Gardiner. Now get yourself on the bloody lorry.'

'But, sir, if the major, or whoever, wants me to take his

photograph, I need all my equipment. I'm sure he'll be none too pleased if I've had to leave most of it behind.'

The rider looked at Ernest with suspicion as if unsure what to do. Then, with a quick dig of his heels into the horse's flank, he wheeled around. The horse reared slightly then stilled.

'Right. Who's your assistant?'

'It's Bill here; he's my assistant.'

'You two chaps, get all your gear together; the lorry leaves in about twenty minutes. I'll clear it with the goddamn sergeant.'

The rider spurred his mount once more and in a cloud of dust rode back down the street in the direction he'd come from.

'Thanks, Ernie,' said Bill, 'but I don't know the first thing about photography.'

'Stick with me, Bill. You'll be all right.'

Bill shoved him hard and both men laughed.

'Right, let's get your equipment then,' said Bill. 'We don't want to miss the transport.'

Ernest picked up his camera and handed Bill the canvas bag. 'Okay, let's go,' he said, and stepped out down the street. He looked back at Bill and started to laugh once more. Bill jogged after him.

'This is it?' he said, a little out of breath. 'This is the equipment?' Bill was laughing now and he put his arm around Ernest's shoulder. 'Come on,' – he mimicked the rider's upper-class accent – 'let's get on that goddamn lorry tout suite, before the sergeant finds out.'

They quickened their pace and proceeded through the

derelict town. The buildings lay shattered and bare; piles of rubble cleared from the roads dwarfed their skeleton brick remains. Chimney stacks stood tall amid the wreckage and window frames jutted at odd angles, defying the gravity that had pulled the rest of the building towards the earth. All about, men sat in twos and threes, smoking and talking, and as Bill and Ernest walked past, the soldiers looked up, curious to know what had caused the spring in their step.

As they turned a ruined corner, they found a darkgreen lorry with a canvas tarpaulin arched over the back. Thick grey smoke belched from its exhaust, obscuring rickety spoked wheels with barely enough tyre to dampen the tiniest of bumps. More than a dozen men sat under the tarpaulin and they moaned and cussed as the additional passengers climbed over the tailgate and assumed the prime position at the back of the vehicle.

Almost as soon as Ernest and Bill had clambered inside, the driver crunched into first gear, and with a couple of loud misfires the lorry lurched forward. The men momentarily lost their balance and tumbled backwards. They grabbed the side rails for stability and found the position they would adopt for the rest of the journey.

Ernest and Bill looked back at the departing town. As the dust cleared they saw the sergeant in hot pursuit. He waved his arms and appeared to be mouthing the words *stop* and *halt* but no sound reached the lorry. Knowing they were safe, they laughed and waved back, both arms high in the air. The sergeant stopped, bent forward and rested his hands on his knees, breathing heavily. When his breath returned he stood, straightened and brushed the dust from his uniform. A small smile broke on his face and he waved, one arm in the air, his hand hardly moving.

'God speed,' he mouthed.

CHAPTER ELEVEN

The Bud

Raymond sat transfixed; his interest and wonder growing as the story progressed.

'So that was my first proper experience of the front line,' said Ernest. 'Bill told me the bits I couldn't remember. You know, those times when I was a quivering wreck' – he shook his head – 'I didn't shower myself in glory, did I?' He picked up his teacup and drained the last drops. 'I wouldn't have got through it if it wasn't for Bill, he's the reason I'm sat here talking to you. He was my friend, and he said everything happened for a reason.' Ernest smiled. 'Maybe he was right.'

'Do you still see him?' asked Raymond.

Ernest looked away; he seemed to hesitate.

'No, we lost touch. Things change.' He raised himself from his chair, using his arms to take the weight off his legs. As he straightened his back, a grimace flashed across his face. He turned to Raymond, then made a point of looking at a gold carriage clock on the mantelpiece. 'Come on,' he said. 'Look at the time. You'd better be off – your mother will be wondering where you are.'

'But I can't go yet,' Raymond said in disbelief. 'We haven't even met Mira!'

Ernest smiled again. 'Tell you what, come again tomorrow and I'll tell you the rest of the story.'

'Promise?'

'Yes, I promise. Now go!'

* * *

Raymond sat on the bus, his head turned to the window as the world whizzed by. A small smile crept over his lips as he stared into space, lost in the afternoon's revelations. Ernest had told him about a different age and he tried to imagine himself uniformed, in a trench, and facing such horrific adversity. How would he have coped? Ernest had been a similar age to him but it was hard to find any empathy with those soldiers – their lives were so different and his own worries seemed trivial in comparison.

The standing passengers swayed to the movement of the packed bus, gripping the silver handrails tightly and reluctantly moving aside as fellow travellers squeezed past, each one alert for a precious empty seat.

The gentle hum of the engine soothed Raymond, and he leant his head against the vibrating glass window, oblivious to the throng surrounding him.

Familiar landmarks began to register, and with a start Raymond realised he was close to home. He sat straight and looked quickly around the bus for the conductor, but she was nowhere to be seen. Shocked into action, and almost without thinking, he stood and excused himself to the passenger next to him, who huffed and angled his knees so Raymond could pass. The red button loomed before him and the reality of his situation dawned. He hesitated, his heart beginning to gallop as he stared hard at the button, willing himself to move. His mind began to scream, dulling all other sound. But then, just as the silence threatened to overwhelm him, he reached forward and pressed the bell.

The familiar ring echoed through the bus and the driver brought the vehicle to a halt. Raymond inched past the standing passengers, hopped off the exit step and stood watching as the bus motored off. He grinned, causing those rarely used muscles in his cheeks to ache. Try as he might he couldn't stop, and as he turned and headed for home, he found himself skipping along the pavement.

He neared his house and saw his garden wall looming into view. Rising above it and slightly swaying were his newly transferred sunflowers. The plants seemed to have grown and were standing straight, pointing towards the sun. Healthy green leaves had replaced the limp pale ones, and as Raymond skipped past his heart missed a beat.

At the top of the tallest flower, a bud had formed. Gently, Raymond drew the stem down towards him and looked more closely, the way Ernest had shown him. Tiny yellow petals were just beginning to emerge from the tight green ball. He felt the blood thumping hard in his head. He allowed the stem to straighten, then ran to the front door. He banged impatiently and, when no one answered, fumbled in his coat pocket for his keys and let himself in.

'Mum, Mum,' he shouted excitedly. 'You'll never guess what.'

Raymond's mother, tea towel in hand, hurried out of the kitchen, her face tight with concern.

'What? What is it Ray?' she said anxiously. 'What's happened? Are you all right?'

'Yes, of course I am. It's my sunflowers – they're coming out!'

'Raymond, I thought you were ill! Where have you been all afternoon?'

'Mum, for the first time ever my sunflowers are actually coming out.' He bounced on his toes in excitement.

'You've been to that old man's, haven't you? I told you to wait until I'd spoken to your dad.' She flicked the tea towel against her leg.

'Mum, he's great. It's because of him my sunflowers are flowering. He said I could be whatever I wanted to be. He ... he ...' In his delight Raymond could find no more words.

'Raymond, what on earth's got into you?' Her lips mirrored his smile.

'I don't know,' said Raymond, turning on the spot. 'I just feel so happy.'

His mother shook her head. 'Oh, Ray, what am I going to do with you?' She tentatively reached forward to touch his arm, but he turned quickly and climbed the stairs.

* * *

That night, Raymond pulled the covers high over his shoulders. It was warm and humid, but he liked the security of the sheltering blankets. Light from the street lamp diffused through his curtains, bathing the bedroom in a golden glow. He began his prayers as usual, wishing his family well, but when he neared the end he paused, thought for a moment, and added, 'And thank you, Lord, for looking after me on the bus and for making it such a good day. Please make tomorrow be just as good. Twenty prayers if tomorrow's just as good. Oh … and, Lord, please look after my friend, Ernest. Amen.'

CHAPTER TWELVE

A Disagreement

The next day, Raymond woke early and wandered downstairs into the kitchen. His father was sitting at the table, reading a newspaper and eating a slice of toast. Raymond tipped some cornflakes into a bowl and sat at the opposite end.

'You're late for work today, Dad,' he said, reaching for the milk.

'I'm working in town today. Cuts out the rail fare, thank goodness. What's happening with you, Ray?'

'I'm going round Ernest's.'

His father frowned. 'Ernest? Do I know him?'

'You know, he was the man I met at the DHSS who helped me with my flowers. He was a photographer in the war.'

'Photographs and flowers won't find you a job, Ray. You need to stop moping around and get yourself out there.' His father hadn't looked up from the paper. 'When are we going to London, anyway?'

'Dad, I'm not moping around.' Raymond's voice rose and his pulse quickened. 'Ernest said we can all do what we want to do. I've been thinking, you remember how I used to get good marks at school for English? Maybe I could be a writer or a journalist.'

'For Christ's sake, Raymond.' His dad slammed the paper down on the table. Raymond jerked, spilling milk and cornflakes. 'All I see you do is walk around with your head down and the weight of the world on your shoulders. And if you're not doing that, you come up with these stupid ideas.' He sipped his tea then continued, 'We can't all do what we *want* to do. Look at me; look at my goddamn awful job. Knuckle down, stop being so miserable and get on with your life. And I can tell you now, you're not seeing that dirty old man again either.'

The chair scraped across the lino as Raymond sprung to his feet. He leant towards his father, fingers stretched out on the table to bear his weight. 'He's not a dirty old man; he's the nicest person I've ever met, and you've told me yourself to find a good job, something I enjoy.'

'That was before. Now you need to live in the real world, and it's not easy.'

Raymond's mum hurried into the kitchen and glanced at her husband and son.

'Now then, what's all this shouting?' she said. 'What on earth's going on?'

'Dad called Ernest a dirty old man and won't let me go round there.'

'I'm sure he didn't mean it. We've just been so worried about you, Ray. Look, how about this; you see Ernest today and then tomorrow you make some phone calls and try to find a job. Is that fair?' She straightened the creases in her apron.

'Yes, Mum,' said Raymond quietly.

His mother turned to her husband. 'I'm sorry, I didn't get the chance to speak to you last night – you were home so late.'

His dad dropped his toast on to the plate and shook his head.

'I can't understand it – yesterday morning you were worried sick about this old bloke.'

'I know, I know, but perhaps I was a little hasty. We shouldn't judge a book by the cover now, should we?' She turned and took the kettle over to the sink. 'Let me make you another cuppa.'

'This family's gone crazy. Perhaps someone would like to help me out when I'm doing a triple overtime shift to make ends meet.' His dad stood and hastily left the table.

'I know, I know,' she said softly. She took a step towards her husband, intent on giving him a hug, but he moved away and into the hall before she could reach him.

'You don't though, that's the trouble,' he called. 'I'm late for work. See you tonight.' They heard him fumble with his coat, then the front door opened and slammed shut.

She sighed. 'Right, Ray, off you go. Don't forget, tomorrow you look for some work to help your dad out. We're just struggling to make ends meet and he's working all the hours under the sun.'

'I will ... I'm sorry, Mum,' said Raymond.

'It'll be all right. We'll get through it – we always do. It's just a bad patch.'

She smiled and reached for Raymond's hand. Feeling awkward, he avoided her touch and squeezed past her and out of the kitchen.

CHAPTER THIRTEEN

Dougal Hyland

Raymond pulled the front door shut and took a deep breath. He hated arguing with his dad but it was something they seemed to be doing more and more. It was as if he had to prove himself and he often felt a disappointment.

He wandered, dejected, down the front path but the bright morning sunshine cheered him and a cool summer breeze revitalised his spirits. Stopping to look at his sunflowers, he smiled. Their stems were even taller and on each there was now a definite bud.

He closed the garden gate behind him and jogged to the bus stop.

The bus was less crowded today and Raymond sat near the front. He watched as the conductor braced herself against the seats, her buttocks clenched either side of the backrest. She shook her satchel to find the correct coppers, then used the handrail to swing acrobatically up the stairs.

He recalled the previous afternoon's events. Did

everything happen for a reason and could he really do anything he wanted as Ernest had said? The ideas, images and future opportunities spiralled in his head like a shoal of glittering golden fish. He smiled, lost in his reverie until, again with surprise, he realised he was nearing his stop. The journey, so often fraught with worry, had simply disappeared.

Although his breath had become shallow and his heart was beating quickly, he gripped the seat in front, reached forward and pressed the bell. The bus slowed and stopped and Raymond leapt off. He felt exhilarated; at that moment any dream was achievable. More than anything else he wanted to share his happiness.

He arrived at Ernest's house and rang the doorbell. A cheerful chime broke the silence followed by a jangle of keys. After what seemed like an age, the older man turned the lock with a satisfying clunk and opened the door. He greeted Raymond warmly and ushered him in.

'It's lovely to see you again,' said Ernest as he moved the cushions from the armchair. 'I didn't think you'd come.' He passed a plate of biscuits. Raymond took a chocolate one.

'Didn't think I'd come? Of course I was going to come.'

He'd taken a bite from the biscuit, and though his mouth was full and he knew it was rude to talk, he couldn't stop himself. The words, and a few crumbs, sprung from his lips, one after the other leaping joyously into the air. 'I've got to hear the end of the story, haven't I?' He picked up a few bits of biscuit from his T-shirt and put them back in his mouth. 'And I've been thinking about all the other things you said as well – you know, the stuff about doing what I want to do. My dad used to say that too. He said he'd help me find something I really enjoyed, but now he just says I've got to be sensible.'

Ernest thought for a moment. 'Well, I suppose he's right, but I still think that if you want to do something more than anything else in the world, if you put every ounce of your heart and soul into it, you can do it. It's just that most people don't have that sort of determination.'

Raymond felt suddenly silly and embarrassed and wished he'd not given voice to his feelings. He studied the room with interest, avoiding Ernest's gaze, the silence broken only by the crunch of biscuits. He was deliberating what to say next when out of nowhere a thought flew into his head. It was now or never – he needed to leap into the unknown and hope that Ernest would be there to catch him. He took a deep breath.

'I ... I think I'd like to write something.'

Ernest laughed and Raymond's cheeks warmed.

'No, no, I'm sorry,' said Ernest. 'I wasn't laughing at your idea, not at all. You just don't sound sure that's all. It doesn't sound like something you want to do more than anything else in the world.'

'Well, I've only just thought of it,' said Raymond defensively, and took another bite of his biscuit. 'I've got to build myself up.'

Ernest's face came alive, like a sea at sunrise, and he broke into silent laughter, his eyes sparkling with joy. Raymond smiled then, glad that he'd brought happiness into the room. He looked into Ernest's kind eyes and saw in them a young man with a life full of dreams.

'Right then,' said Ernest. 'You'll need your writer's name; you can't be Raymond Mann, even though that's a very good name. Did you ever have a pet?'

'Yes, I had a dog. Dougal. She was great but we couldn't train her and she kept running away.' He smiled as he remembered.

'She?'

'Yeah, well, we got her from Petticoat Lane Market in London and the man told my dad she was a cairn terrier and a boy. It turned out she was a Heinz 57 and a girl; we didn't know much about dogs,' he said sadly, shaking his head.

Raymond glanced at Ernest, who was trying not to laugh. He lost the battle and an explosive chuckle burst from his clenched lips.

'Right, that's your first name,' said Ernest composing himself. 'Now, what was your mother's maiden name?'

'Hyland,' said Raymond.

'Perfect – your writer's name is Dougal Hyland.' Ernest raised a chocolate biscuit in salute. 'May we welcome Dougal Hyland to the pantheon of writers who have moved and astounded us, made us think, taken us away from our daily drudgery, and with just a pen and paper changed the world.' He tapped his biscuit against Raymond's and laughed.

Spellbound, Raymond could only sit and stare at the tiny yellow crumbs that fell from the biscuits and bounced on to the coffee table.

'Right, I suppose you want to hear some more of my story. Remind me, where was I?'

'Well, you'd just left on the lorry and the sergeant was none too pleased.'

'Ah, yes,' said Ernest. 'Well, we didn't know it at the time but we were heading for a town called Bailleul, which we'd occupied since 1914. It had become an important hospital centre where the casualties went before returning home to England.' He settled back on the sofa and closed his eyes. 'Bailleul had also become our headquarters and a rather dashing chap called General Babcock-Billiaire felt his war efforts should be captured on film for the nation.' Ernest chuckled. 'My camera, rather than me, was closest to him so that's why they wanted me there urgently. The town was near the front, but it hadn't seen action for a while and many of the local women were still working the fields. That's how I met Mira.' He smiled and turned his head towards Raymond. 'But before I carry on, let me get us some tea.'

CHAPTER FOURTEEN

Ernest's Story (Part Two)

1917

The green lorry bumped along the winding track; its tiny tyres and inefficient suspension gave the men little protection from the ruts in the road. Frequent groans splintered the silence as potholes jarred their backs and bounced them off their seats. A trail of red dust marked the vehicle's progress and mingled with the cloudy white exhaust fumes that pumped into the air with each misfire.

Bill and Ernest were still in a state of euphoria, buoyed by their good fortune. Time and again their eyes met and they fell into fits of laughter, much to the bemusement and annoyance of their travelling companions.

The truck followed the narrow road through seemingly never-ending fields of vibrant blue and gold. Small dirt tracks led to long abandoned farmhouses and vast untended cornfields. Bright sunlight shone through the trees, dazzling the men as the thick branches momentarily caged then released the rays. Occasionally they would meet a column of soldiers or another truck heading in the opposite direction. Raucous jeers and obscene waves would ensue, but apart from those brief interludes, Bill and Ernest found themselves lost in the rhythm of the lorry, and the morning crawled into the afternoon.

The truck slowed and then tipped as it traversed a small humpbacked bridge. The men looked down over the stone parapet into the crystal-clear water of a fast-flowing stream, the reflected light etching their half-closed eyelids with silver sparkles.

The truck reached the apex and began to tilt the other way. Happy childlike groans filled the air as the soldier's stomachs fluttered. On the other side of the bridge, a group of women laundered clothes on the far bank of the stream, their long skirts tucked into waistbands. Soap bubbles billowed around them and bobbed down the river, occasionally floating into the air, the only clouds in a clear blue sky.

Ernest raised his hand to shield his eyes. Its shadow settled on his face and the dazzling light relented. One of the women stopped her scrubbing and looked up at him. She'd tied back her long dark hair, but a few strands had fallen over her cheek and she brushed them aside with a wet hand. Her white shirt was open and Ernest saw perspiration glistening on her neck. She smiled, stilling the world. Ernest watched breathless, aware that any movement would break the spell.

The truck trundled on and the bridge receded but

Ernest's gaze remained towards the stream, his face aglow and his smile endless. Bill dug him in the ribs.

'Hey, Ernie, what a woman. And someone to do your washing too.'

The men laughed and Bill waved his hands, whistling and shouting.

Woken from his reverie, Ernest stood and grabbed Bill's arms to stop him drawing the women's attention, but Bill playfully pushed him aside just as the truck turned a corner. Ernest overbalanced and fell headlong to the dusty wooden floor. On all fours amongst a multitude of legs, his embarrassment doubled as laughter pealed from his companions. He took a deep breath and, with only his head visible above the tailgate, he dared to look back at the stream before the bend in the road obscured his view forever.

To his astonishment and joy, the woman was still looking and still smiling.

The scenery changed and grey roads and dark broken dwellings replaced the green fields and red dirt tracks. A thoughtful silence descended within the lorry as it reached the outskirts of the town, but the men's mood lifted as the buildings became brighter and in better repair. It soon became clear that this was a lively place with lorries arriving and departing every few minutes, depositing stretchers outside impressive premises adorned with huge Red Cross signs. Civilians mingled with the military, and nurses hurried about their duties in twos and threes. Laughter and the low murmur of conversation emanated from the buildings. Bill and Ernest looked upon the town with interest – it was so different to the one they'd left with its broken blackened husks.

The lorry slowed and came to a juddering halt outside a large building that might once have been the town hall. Palatial steps led up to solid wooden doors and a large Union Jack fluttered above.

The men lowered themselves from the truck, dusted their uniforms with enthusiastic slaps and stretched their aching limbs.

A corporal ran down the steps and into the melee of men.

'Who's the photographer? Who's the photographer?' he shouted, pushing through the crowd. He wore a re-signed expression as if expecting his question to be met by silence.

'That's us,' said Bill, grinning. 'We're ready to create our masterpiece.'

The corporal stopped and looked at Bill and Ernest; he exhaled and seemed to grow taller, as if a great weight had been lifted from him.

'Really?' he said. 'Right, this way. Follow me.'

'Hold your horses,' said Bill, putting his arm around Ernest and straightening him. 'Ernie here is your artistic type. He's a bit sensitive, and after that long trip he'll need a bath and something to eat before he can think about photographs.'

'Well, good luck with that,' said the corporal, hurrying ahead. 'I'll let you tell the general, but my orders are to bring you to him as soon as you get here and this is the third bloody lorry you're supposed to be on, so you're already late. I was beginning to think you weren't coming.'

The corporal led the way up the steps and through heavy wooden doors. Although the town was busy, Bill and Ernest were not prepared for the pandemonium that greeted them inside the building. Officers dodged and jostled as they endeavoured to get to their destinations.

There were maps everywhere – large ones hung on every inch of wall, while smaller charts had been spread over desks surrounded by a huddle of men moving dark blocks and identifying places of interest with long wooden pointers. The tobacco smoke from what seemed like a thousand pipes and cigarettes was funnelled into grey columns by the shafts of sunlight that shone through the tall windows.

They followed their guide through several rooms and up two flights of stairs until they reached a dark oak door at the end of a long corridor. The corporal knocked twice.

'General Babcock-Billiaire, sir, the photographers are here.'

Bill and Ernest looked at each other and mouthed the general's name. Ernest put his hand over his mouth to stifle his laughter. The corporal saw the gesture and gave an urgent and barely perceptible shake of his head.

'Enter.' A loud confident baritone boomed from the room.

The corporal opened the door and ushered in the two dusty men. It was like stepping into an English stately home; large pictures of heroic soldiers on horseback adorned the dark, wood-panelled walls. Chairs and tables of different sizes, shapes and shades filled every open space and ornaments and table lamps cluttered the room further. A large oblong rug depicting an African hunting scene was just visible on the floor; it led to an impressive desk behind which sat a soldier of over-stated importance. He wore a full-dress uniform, the scarlet bright against the dark of the room. Across his chest a row of overlapping medals added to the pomp. The golden waistband, tassels and scrambled-egg piping around the sleeves and shoulders of the uniform complemented his slicked-back chestnut hair. He was well built and strong, though the buttons on his tunic struggled over a growing paunch and the pink tinge of his nose and cheeks betrayed a love of good food and wine that his small greying moustache failed to hide.

Ernest and Bill walked up to the desk and saluted.

'Afternoon, gentleman. I'm so pleased to see you. I can't tell you what a bloody bore it's been waiting around in this godforsaken town.' The general spoke with an upper-class and privileged accent. He ran his fingers through his oily hair. 'What a command to get … casualties! Can you believe it? Me, General Babcock-Billiaire, having to sort out a bunch of cowards who shot themselves rather than fighting the bloody Hun. I can't even remember the last time I sent my boys over the top – that's what they love, you know.' The general waved his hands and his face reddened. 'Honour and sacrifice – my boys wouldn't have ended up here. Well, apart from bloody Wilkins, but we shot him ourselves, anyway.'

The corporal glanced at Bill and Ernest and widened his eyes.

'Right, now, as you can see, I'm dressed and ready for action. I've been waiting here for bloody ages.' The general stood and straightened his jacket. 'Let's take some pictures. We'll show those blasted pen-pushers back home I'm still a bloody hero.' The general walked past the three men. 'The Hun has given us an opportunity to capture – in a simple but glorious photograph – all the qualities that make our nation great. I shall be centre stage, of course, standing astride a trench, or perhaps lending a hand to a fallen comrade, or pointing my rifle at the Bosch or' – the general's voice rose with his increasing excitement – 'or staring majestically into the sky, thinking of home.' He looked heavenwards.

'Or on horseback, sir,' said Bill.

'What?' The general's small, beady eyes settled on Bill.

'Look at all these pictures on your walls, sir, and think of those magnificent statues in London. All the great men are on horseback; you'll be continuing the tradition, but in a modern way. Ernie here is an artist – he can do anything with a camera.'

The general was silent for a few moments as he considered the proposal.

'Yes, yes, *yes!*' He banged his fist on the table, making Ernest and the corporal flinch.

'I knew this was the right decision. You see what I mean, Corporal? These men are professionals.' The general strode past them. 'Right, when can we start? I'm ready now. Corporal, get me a horse! NOW. What are you waiting for, you lazy bloody idiot?'

'Oh, I'm sorry, sir,' said Bill.

'Yes, yes, what is it, man?'

'Well, it's Ernie here, sir. He needs to prepare his, er, plates. That's right, Ernie, isn't it?'

Ernest looked at the floor, feigning interest in the carpet. 'Um, er, yes. I have to get the plates ready,' he mumbled.

The general stopped in front of them, irritated. 'Well, how long? When can we start?'

'It'll take two or three days I reckon, sir. Isn't that right, Ernie?'

Ernest had not looked up.

'Um, yes,' he said again, quietly.

The general huffed, making no effort to hide his agitation. 'What's the matter with you, man?' He raised his voice and looked at Ernest. 'Can't you speak?'

Bill stepped forward. 'Like I said, sir, he's an artist – a little sensitive. His last mission was behind enemy lines, taking pictures of the trenches; he barely got out alive. He broke his camera on a Hun's head.'

Ernest's own head jerked up and he stared at Bill in disbelief, but Bill was in full flow.

'What he needs, sir, is somewhere quiet to prepare his photographic plates. And he hasn't eaten for two days because of his experiences. Look, his hands are shaking through lack of food and that's no good for a photographer, you know. Show the general your hands, Ernie.'

Ernest looked imploringly at Bill, his eyes wide. He mouthed a small *no*.

'That's it, Ernie. Don't be shy.'

Bill coughed, though Ernest wondered whether he wasn't suppressing a laugh.

Ernest raised his hands, all the time staring at Bill, and began to shake his fingers slowly.

'Good God, man, what you must have been through. Behind enemy lines, you say?' The general patted Ernest on the back so hard that he had to take a step forward to keep his balance. 'You see, Corporal? These are real men not bloody secretaries; they have the hearts of lions.'

The corporal looked at Bill and Ernest, barely disguising his anger.

The general scratched his chin. 'You must tell me more about these adventures over dinner. In the meantime, Corporal, see that these men are billeted in suitable officer accommodation and make sure they receive all they need; I'm holding you personally responsible for his shaking hands. They need to be still by the time he takes my photograph.'

'B-But, sir—'

'Dismissed. I'll see you in three days.' He turned back to his desk. 'And, Corporal, find me a bloody horse. I'm a superb rider but it needs to stand still for the photograph so you'd better make sure it's bloody placid.'

Bill and Ernest followed the corporal down the wide flight of stairs, through the gaggle of officers and out on to the street. The bright sunshine left them stunned after the dark, smoke-filled rooms, and Ernest could barely stop himself from leaping in the air. His stride resembled a hop as he bounced along the pavement in excitement.

'What do you mean, sensitive artist?' he said.

Bill laughed. 'I've got to look after you, Ernie boy. You've been behind enemy lines. Look at your hands shaking.'

Ernest raised his hands and chased Bill down the street, arms outstretched, zombie-like. He aimed a kick but Bill dodged and ran ahead.

'I told you, stick with me, Ernie, and you'll be okay,' said Bill, waving the camera bag.

The corporal turned around sharply. 'Stop arsing about,' he said crossly. 'I'm already in enough bloody trouble cos of you two dingbats. We've got to get to a farmhouse before nightfall or I'll never find my way back. And for Christ's sake, look after your camera. The general will have me shot if this goes wrong.' He shook his head in exasperation as Bill and Ernest continued to chase each other. 'And you think I'm sodding joking, you bloody idiots!' he shouted desperately.

Ernest and Bill sheepishly fell back in line. The three men continued in silence down the street until they reached a large town square surrounded by tall, imposing buildings. A group of Australian soldiers were playing football in the centre, chasing a heavy leather ball. Their tanned bodies and unfamiliar accents seemed strange and out of place in the quaint market square. A few British soldiers were watching the match, leaning against the statues, their trousers and shirt sleeves rolled up, enjoying the last of the sun's rays. They offered the players ever more obscene advice as the game progressed and their raucous laughter echoed around the buildings along with the thud of the ball.

'Bloody Aussies,' said the corporal. 'I hate 'em, bigheaded bastards. They got a casualty-clearing centre up by the railway and they still come down here to our patch to play. They got it easy.'

A shrill windy whistle cut through the air and a plume of dirty white smoke rose above the buildings. A train pulled into the town station. A few minutes later the chug and strain of another, heading in the opposite direction, momentarily drowned out the shouts of the footballers and their spectators.

'Poor buggers,' said the corporal. 'Probably half-dead but at least they only copped a Blighty and can get home now.'

The streets narrowed and the shadows lengthened, but the town remained a bustling hive of activity, with lorries and horse-drawn carts coming and going in quick succession. The Red Cross had commandeered many of the buildings as holding areas for the wounded before their transfer back to England and stretcher-bearers jogged down side streets, taking short cuts to speed their journeys. Columns of men waited patiently to be called to the station, their faces masks of uncertainty, not sure where the next train would take them.

Despite this, Bill and Ernest felt relaxed, and they strolled along the walkways as if on holiday, taking in the scenery and breathing the cool dry air, so different to the clogging damp of the front-line trenches. They remained oblivious to the corporal's tuts and constant efforts to speed them up.

As the orange glow of twilight descended over the town, the paved walkways gave way to dirt tracks. The men arrived at a rickety wooden gate blocking the path to a neglected thatched farmhouse.

The corporal bounded through the gate, happy to have reached his destination. He banged hard on the sturdy old weather-beaten door. When there was no reply he repeated his knock with even more gusto.

'Open up,' he shouted.

There was a creak of floorboards and the door opened a couple of inches. Through the crack a single shadowed eye scrutinised them. The door opened a little more, scraping on the wooden floor. A middle-aged woman in a long, light-blue dress and a faded yellow headscarf stood in the hallway. Her auburn hair fell over her leathery face and onto plump shoulders.

Ernest peered over the corporal's shoulder, thinking the woman was probably much younger than she'd first appeared.

Her hands shook as she gripped the door but instead of moving aside to let them in she held her head high and her mouth taut and defiant.

'Right in you go.' The corporal motioned with a nod of his head to Bill and Ernest. They remained still and looked at each other in embarrassment.

'For Christ's sake, get in. I haven't got all sodding night.' The corporal forced the door open with a quick kick that jarred the woman's fingers.

Bill and Ernest squeezed past and mumbled an apology.

The corporal turned to the woman and spoke slowly and loudly. 'These men will be staying with you for a while. You must feed them and find them somewhere to sleep.'

The woman took a step backwards and shook her head; she looked frightened and confused.

'Sodding hell,' hissed the corporal. 'Fucking frogs. Thick as two short planks. DO YOU UNDERSTAND?'

Bill came back to the door and spoke softly in French. The woman nodded curtly but seemed to relax and moved inside the hallway.

'Right, see you both in a couple of days,' said the corporal, relieved. 'You'd better be as good as the general thinks you are or we're all bloody well done for.'

The woman closed the door and with a tiny movement of her hand led them down the hallway.

'What did you say to her?' whispered Ernest.

'Oh, I apologised and explained what we're doing here and, er ...' Bill grinned. 'Well, I may have just mentioned you recently took some photos of the royal family.'

'*What?* Bill!' Ernest shook his head but was unable to stop a smile spreading over his face. 'Where did you learn to speak French, anyway?'

'My mother was French; it comes in handy sometimes. But don't tell the general or he'll have me doing all sorts of missions.'

The woman led them up a flight of steep, narrow stairs that groaned under the additional weight. At the top was a long landing with several doors leading off. The woman opened the nearest one and beckoned the men inside before lighting two candles that bathed the room in a flickering yellow light. It was a small room with two beds, each set against a wall. At the end was a fireplace with a stone hearth. The beds looked comfortable and inviting, with plump white pillows and soft yellow bedspreads.

It was quiet; a cosy haven of peace.

Bill and Ernest looked at each other, not quite believing their luck; it had been many months since they'd slept in a proper bed. The woman left the room and the door creaked shut behind her.

'Beats the trenches, Ernie,' said Bill. 'I told you—'

'Yes, I know, stick with you and I'll be all right.' Ernest laughed.

Bill moved to the nearest bed and in one quick movement flung his feet outwards and leapt backwards on to it with a thud.

'Shhhhh, careful,' hissed Ernest, but Bill was already curling into a ball, his head disappearing into the soft pillow. Ernest looked at his own bed. The temptation to lie down was overwhelming, but something made him open the bedroom door and look down the landing. 'I'm going for a wander,' he said.

'You won't see anything in the dark,' said Bill, stifling a yawn. 'Get your head down, mate.'

'I know. I just fancy doing a bit of exploring,'

Ernest closed the door behind him, found the narrow staircase and gingerly made his way down the creaking steps, all the while clutching the thick rope handrail. Only a dim orange glow illuminated the walls, and he almost tripped over a portly black cat that attempted to wrap itself around his legs. Slowly his eyes grew accustomed to the darkness and he began to move with more confidence.

He reached the hallway and saw light from a doorway halfway down the corridor. He moved towards it and found himself in the kitchen; it was lit by flickering candles strategically placed on the tables.

The woman stood by the sink. She turned, smiled and beckoned him over. Beside her on an old oak butcher's block was a large crusty loaf of bread cut in two, crispy golden crumbs scattered around it. The woman picked up a knife, cut a generous slice and held it towards him. Ernest stepped into the room and took the bread, not knowing what to say or how to say it. He felt a blush forming on his face and hoped the woman wouldn't notice in the candlelight.

'Thank you,' he mumbled, staring at the floor. 'Merci.'

The woman smiled and waved her hand, beckoning him to look around. The bread was still warm and as he bit, the crust crunched in his mouth. Ernest closed his eyes, savouring the taste and the texture.

The kitchen was homely. Ernest thought it had probably remained unchanged for many years. A large wooden table in the middle of the room was surrounded by an assortment of chairs and stools. The seat at the farthest end had a high rounded back and worn arm rests. It stood ready for the head of the house, a clean plate and cutlery laid before it.

Hanging from a square wooden frame attached to the ceiling by rusting black chains was a collection of pots, pans and other cooking implements. The candlelight cast long shadows on the walls, making it difficult to discern how big the kitchen really was, but Ernest nodded to the woman and continued his exploration. A thin red chequered cloth covered the lattice window of a small white back door. Through the curtain he could see the glow of more dancing candles. He opened the door gently, just enough to peek through to the garden beyond. His eyes fell instantly upon the woman who'd waved to him earlier from the river, and the shock of recognition left him disorientated. He breathed a tiny gasp and goose bumps tingled on his arms and legs as his heart quickened.

His initial impulse was to close the door, but he stood transfixed. She was the most beautiful woman he'd ever seen in his young life. She sat on a wicker sofa at the far end of a long wooden veranda, her head turned away from him. She'd been reading by the candlelight but now stared into the night sky, wistful and lost. The yellow glow illuminated her long elegant neck and her black hair shimmered silver in the moonlight. As Ernest pushed the door a fraction wider a floor board creaked beneath his feet. Startled, the woman turned her head towards him.

If Helen had launched a thousand ships, then this face would have launched a thousand more, Ernest was sure.

He remained frozen in the doorway, unable to breathe. In that second it was as if the moonlight existed only for her and as she turned, her pale face became framed by her long dark hair and an eternity of stars. Ernest felt weak, his fingers turning white as they gripped the door frame. Their eyes met. Then she smiled and a shooting star soared behind her, lighting up the night sky before disappearing beneath the deep waves of her hair.

Ernest's heart was beating so quickly he was sure his chest was about to explode. And in that moment, the dreariness and fear that had filled his days dissolved.

'Bonjour,' said the woman quietly. She was still smiling.

'Bon ... bonjour. I'm afraid I don't speak any French.

Can you speak English?' He pushed open the door so she could see him but remained in the kitchen.

The woman laughed gently. 'Oui, er, yes. I mean a little. Look, I am reading English poetry.' She held up a book. 'Come, sit next to me. My name is Mirabelle, but please call me Mira. My mother said we had two Tommies staying with us.' Mira moved to the side of the sofa to make room for him. 'I saw you on the lorry?'

Ernest stepped onto the veranda. Her eyes followed him and he felt self-conscious, unable to remember how he normally held his arms.

'Yes, that was me,' said Ernest, moving to the wicker sofa. 'I'm Ernest Gardiner but Ernie will do. That's what my friend Bill calls me.'

'Oh no. Mirabelle is a crazy name – it's too long – but Ernest is wonderful, a powerful name.' She patted the sofa. 'Please sit. Is your friend from the lorry here as well? He was funny.'

'Yes, he's here. He's asleep upstairs.' Ernest sat down next to Mira, wondering if she was mocking him. He pretended to concentrate on something in the far distance as she looked intently at his profile. She smiled as if aware of his shyness.

'Do you live here?' said Ernest, desperate for something to say.

Mira laughed. 'Yes of course. That is my mother in the kitchen.' She shook her head and looked away. 'My father is fighting with your Tommies. We have not heard from him for two months; we are so worried ... and ... and ... my sweetheart was killed at the start of the war and we hear the dreadful news.' Her voice cracked as she spoke and Ernest turned to look at her.

'I'm sorry,' he said. 'It must be so hard for you.'

'Merci, but it is hard for all of us and you are so young.'

'I'm not that young,' said Ernest a little more quickly and sharply than he had intended. 'I'm eighteen, well nearly. Anyway, I'm a soldier and …' The heat rose again to his cheeks.

'Pardon me, Ernest. You are indeed a brave young man, but your eyes should not be seeing this misery. Your life should be filled with colours and joy and you should be held safe in your mother's arms.'

Mira shivered and quickly took his hand in hers. Ernest started to pull away but the tender touch of her soft warm skin felt beautiful and, against all his instincts, he allowed his hand to remain clasped in hers.

'I'm sorry, I shouldn't be saying those things, but I am so worried about my father,' she said. Then, with a child-like gasp, she nudged Ernest. 'Look! Look at the sky.' Two shooting stars glided gracefully across the dark canopy. 'There is so much beauty in the world. Look – a sky full of stars, but there's so little hope at the moment.'

'It's beautiful,' whispered Ernest shyly, 'and I know what you mean – everything seems awful right now, but I'm sure there's still hope and I know your father will be home soon.' He now felt more at ease and was suddenly overcome by a need to offload the emotions he had hidden for so long. 'I shouldn't say this either but every day I wish I hadn't signed up. I heard the stories and saw the women giving out white feathers; I just didn't want them to think I was frightened.'

'Are you frightened?'

Ernest turned away as his eyes began to sting.

'All the time,' he said quietly. He looked down at the books in Mira's lap, wanting to talk about something, anything else. 'Tell me about your book.'

Mira smiled. 'Which one?' she picked up an olive-green notebook. 'This one is my journal. Each evening I write down my thoughts and memories of the day. And this,' she said, replacing it with a small, black cloth-bound book, 'is my poetry book. My father bought it for me; he thought it would help improve my English. It is full of your poetry, but difficult to understand. I think lots of the poems are old and written many years ago.' She turned the pages, momentarily lost in thought. 'I am reading William Wordsworth at the moment.'

'Would you read it?' said Ernest. 'I don't know anything about William Wordsworth, but it would be nice to hear you speak.'

Mira gently let go of Ernest's hand. 'Yes, of course, but it seems strange – me, a French peasant teaching a young English gentleman about his poetry.'

They both laughed.

'I'm afraid I'm not from the gentry,' he said. 'What poem is it?'

Mira turned to him and put her feet on the sofa, bending her knees so she could prop the book against them. She moved her head closer and fanned through the pages.

Ernest could only stare in wonder and admiration as the candlelight danced across her face. He smiled as a frown of concentration tightened her brow and the breeze teased a strand of dark hair across her face. It was so peaceful beneath the stars – unreal, like a dream; a different world to the terror of the trenches. His eyes followed the contours of her neck downwards until the delicate swell of her breasts, rising and falling with each breath, gently captured his gaze.

Mira cleared her throat and with a start Ernest's eyes found hers. Embarrassed, he hoped she'd not think badly of him but as their eyes met, he found only lines of laughter on her face as she once again graced him with her soft smile.

She began to read.

> 'Surprised by joy – impatient as the wind,
> I turned to share the transport – Oh! With whom,
> But thee, long buried in the silent tomb,
> That spot which no vicissitude can find?
> Love, faithful love, recalled thee to my mind –
> But how could I forget thee? – Through what
>   power,
> Even for the least division of an hour,
> Have I been so beguiled as to be blind
> To my most grievous loss! – That thought's return
> Was the worst pang that sorrow ever bore,
> Save one, one only, when I stood forlorn,
> Knowing my heart's best treasure was no more;
> That neither present time, nor years unborn
> Could to my sight that heavenly face restore.'

Mira sighed and closed her eyes. 'Such beautiful words, but so sad.'

Ernest thought he saw a tiny tear shining in the corner

of Mira's eye, but the flickering light made it impossible to be sure.

Miles from the mud and the mayhem, beguiled by this voice that sung so softly, Ernest lost himself. Mira touched his hand and then gently held the tips of his fingers. Joy burst within him, spiralling down his spine and then onwards to every long-neglected outpost of his body.

The back door banged shut.

Ernest jumped and straightened, releasing Mira's hand. He looked up; Bill stood before them.

'Ernie, you sly old dog! No wonder you've been so quiet.' Bill laughed, winked and sat down on a brown wooden chair to the side of them.

'Hello, Bill,' said Ernest nervously. 'This is Mira. Mira, this is my best mate, Bill. He saved my life and got me through this war so far; I wouldn't be here without him.' He smiled shyly at Bill.

'Ah, shut up, mate. You'll be hugging me next.' Bill laughed and looked at Mira. 'Gentil de vous recontrer. Comment allez vous, Mira?'

'Goodness, an Englishman who can speak French. Quand les poules auront des dents.' Mira turned to Ernest. 'Sorry, I said it is as rare as a hen with teeth.' Mira laughed. 'Where did you learn?' she asked Bill.

'My mother was French,' said Bill, 'so I grew up speaking both languages.'

'Well, it is nice to meet you. I can speak simple English, and it is good to practise. Talking to Ernest has been lovely.' She reached over and squeezed his fingers. Ernest, shocked by the familiarity, withdrew his hand quickly and glanced over at Bill, who was trying, unsuccessfully, not to laugh.

'Are you hungry?' said Mira. 'I know my mother has bread and cheese in the kitchen.' She stood up, straightened her dress and put the books down on a small table near the sofa. 'Come on,' she said, reaching for the door.

The two men stood and let Mira pass. Bill beckoned for Ernest to go next. As Ernest moved in front, Bill pushed him in the back, laughing. When Ernest turned, Bill used his hands to mime the shape of a voluptuous woman.

Shut up, Ernest mouthed, smiling.

CHAPTER FIFTEEN

The Escape

1972

Ernest had stopped talking and Raymond was surprised and saddened to see tears running down the old man's face.

'Ernest, what's the matter?' he asked.

'Oh, it's nothing, just memories – such beautiful times mixed with such terror. I wish everyone in the world could experience how I felt when I first saw Mira. I'm sure war, terrorism and religion would all fade away if people could feel the joy I did that night.' Ernest took a large white handkerchief, wiped his eyes and blew his nose.

'What happened after that?' said Raymond. 'Did you take the photograph?'

'Well' – Ernest leant sideways to stuff the handkerchief back in his pocket and compose himself – 'we spent the next couple of weeks at Mira's house, and I fell more and more in love with her. She read other poems, but that first one has always stuck with me and it's still my favourite. "My heart's best treasure" – what a beautiful line.'

The afternoon sun passed behind dark clouds, and a grey shadow settled across the room.

'The three of us had a wonderful time; we were always together and there was never a hint of jealousy; we just became inseparable.' Ernest chuckled. 'Though as the youngest by quite a few years, I was often the butt of their jokes. The general was happy with his photograph and I also took the picture of Mira you saw on the hall table.'

Ernest stared over to the photograph of the line of troops.

'Then, as quickly as our friendship started, it finished. Bill and I got billeted a couple of miles away from Mira and, despite the usual promises to stay in touch, we drifted apart. There was about a year left of the war and we lived it out peacefully in Bailleul, working at the casualty clearing station. We were very lucky.'

Ernest eased himself from his chair. 'Listen, I've told you enough, and it's getting late. You'd better be off.' He led the way through the living room, then stopped and turned to Raymond. 'Tomorrow's my favourite night of the year. It's the Perseid meteor shower. Can you get round here at about eleven? We can watch it together.'

'Eleven? You mean eleven o'clock at night? My mum will never let me out that late. And how would I get here anyway? There aren't any buses.' Raymond shook his head and shrugged. 'What is it anyway?'

Ernest laughed. 'Well, if you don't know I won't spoil

the surprise. Maybe I could come and pick you up.' He opened the front door. 'If you can't get out, just look up at the stars around midnight – it's supposed to be the best display for years.'

* * *

Raymond sat on the bus, watching the familiar streets drift past and thinking about the afternoon's events. He thought about Bill and Mira and what their lives had been like, and wondered whether the photograph of the general still existed. He tried to imagine how Ernest had felt that night, and whether he'd ever fall in love himself.

The bus stopped and the ritual rut of passengers leaving and joining ensued. Someone sat in the empty seat next to Raymond and squeezed him against the window. He shifted his position and turned to look at the person. A smiling, spotty face only inches from his own returned his gaze.

'Hello, Mr Bender,' the man whispered, low and menacing.

Raymond felt the icy spark of recognition; it was one of the thugs from the dole office. Without thinking he began to stand. A hand on his shoulder pushed him back into his seat; then came a hard flick to the back of his head. Raymond looked around, horrified to see another of the youths sitting behind him.

'I'm sure this isn't your stop just yet,' the skinhead said with a laugh.

Raymond rubbed his head and sat. Panic rose in his

chest. He knew his breathing would soon falter, but he was desperate not to show any weakness.

'Leave me alone,' he said. 'I need to get off anyway.'

'Now now, no need to be nasty. We were just wondering about your old boyfriend. Is he still alive?' the skinhead hissed, spit wetting Raymond's face. 'I hope you haven't shagged him to death, you fucking bum plumbers.'

'I don't know who you mean.' Raymond's arms shook and he was no longer sure his legs would take his weight. 'I've got to get off here.'

'Really? Oh, what a stroke of luck – this is our stop too.' The yob next to Raymond grinned and nodded his head.

He stood up quickly and forced his way past the skinhead's stubborn legs. The conductor rang the bell and Raymond leapt off the bus before it had fully come to a halt. He walked as fast as he could, determined not to run, staring straight ahead. He could hear heavy footsteps echoing on the pavement and knew the yobs were walking close behind, mimicking him. Something tapped his foot, pushing it behind his calf. He stumbled and took a large stride, his arms outstretched to keep his balance, but he continued on stubbornly. There was laughter behind him, and then another trip, this one sending him sprawling.

More laughter.

'Whoops, sorry about that, Mr Bender.'

Raymond got to his feet, his hands grazed and stinging. He looked down. There was a dirty jagged tear in his jeans where his knee had hit the pavement. He took a deep breath. It caught in his throat and he walked forwards again.

The two skinheads continued to follow, then danced in front of him, blocking his path.

'Don't run away, Mr Bender. We just want to have a friendly chat. That old codger could have killed me. We want to know where he lives. You tell us and we'll let you off.' The yob took hold of Raymond's wrist, his fingers easily encircling it, and lifted his arm above his head, stretching his body. Raymond tried to twist away but the skinhead was too strong.

'Let me go,' Raymond moaned, his voice becoming higher. There seemed no escape from his humiliation. He gulped for air and a desperate sob escaped his throat. The skinheads laughed.

'You fucking little poofter, we're going to beat the crap out of you.' They twisted Raymond's arm, pirouetting him on the spot. 'That's it, dance for us, bender. I expect the old codger likes you to do that.'

One of the thugs punched Raymond hard in the stomach, forcing the air from his lungs. His legs collapsed beneath him and the skinhead, unable to hold him upright, let go of his arm. He fell on to the hard pavement and curled into a ball.

A memory of football on a cold November morning fluttered into his mind. Rick 'Jock Strap' Derris, the star of the school team, had kicked the ball at point-blank range into Raymond's stomach. For several seconds, Raymond had thought he'd be all right. Then pain, deep and dark, had torn through his gut and into his chest. He'd crumpled to the floor and his teammates had crowded around, laughing and prodding his prone body until a whistle blew and the teacher helped him to his feet.

The class were sent back to the changing rooms. In that stark, stone-clad room with its wooden benches and embarrassing showers, he'd tried to button his shirt, but his fingers were so numb with cold that he couldn't get them to work. He'd gone to his next lesson with his shirt open; displaying the ridiculous string vest his mum had made him wear. The taunts lasted for the whole term and had been far harder to bear than the pain inflicted by the football.

Now, here on the cold pavement, that wretched feeling of humiliation overwhelmed him again. He couldn't get his breath and he was drowning, retching as the pain overwhelmed him. Between snot-filled sobs he choked on the dust from the dirty concrete. Footsteps from passers-by, doggedly looking the other way, boomed through his skull.

The skinhead took hold of Raymond's hair and dragged him to his knees.

'Where's the old bender live?' he snarled. 'If you don't tell us, then we'll have to sort you out instead.' His clenched fist hovered close to Raymond's nose.

Raymond could only gulp between shallow breaths and each time he tried to talk he was shamed by his sobs.

One of the skinheads pulled him roughly to his feet and forced him to stand against a wall. The other held his throat and pushed his neck firmly back against the brickwork.

'Last chance,' he said, kneeing Raymond in the thigh, aiming for a dead leg.

Raymond's endurance was at an end; he took a deep, deep breath. 'His address is in my wallet,' he gasped.

'That's better,' said the skinhead in mock gratitude, releasing Raymond's throat and brushing some of the dust off his shoulders.

Raymond inched away from the wall and slowly reached for his back pocket. His home was two hundred yards away. He'd never been very good at running but it was a chance.

He bolted.

His arms pumped furiously and while his legs seemed to move in slow motion, he'd covered thirty yards before the skinheads had realised what was happening.

They exploded into movement, greyhounds in pursuit of an injured hare, shouting, swearing and dodging unsuspecting pedestrians. Raymond skidded around a corner, narrowly missing a mother and toddler. He glanced behind; his pursuers were gaining ground. His heart galloped and, desperate, he tried to increase his pace. His goal was close and he put every ounce of effort into reaching it, hoping the yobs might save something for a longer chase.

'You better stop, you fucking bender, or you're dead,' they shouted.

Raymond accelerated, focusing on nothing but survival. He saw his house in the distance and his legs found a rhythm that surprised him. The skinheads' footsteps pounded behind him, but Raymond dared not take another look.

Just as his lungs were about to explode and his legs

buckle, he reached the garden gate, forced it open, ran up the path and collapsed against the front door.

He beat hard and fast on it with open hands. 'Mum, *Mum*, open the door.'

The door remained shut.

The skinheads had reached the house and strode up the path towards him.

'Well, Mr Bender, we warned you. Now … you're gonna get your fucking head kicked in!' They chanted the words football-style and laughed.

The front door opened and Raymond's mother appeared.

'What on earth's going on?' she said, startled by the commotion. She stood with her hands on her hips and her cheeks flushed. 'You two, off my property this instant, before I call the police.'

The skinheads stopped in their tracks.

'Off! *Now!*'

'Oh, fuck, it's Bender's mum come to look after him. You fucking poof, Bender. You tell us where the old pervert lives or you're dead.'

The skinheads ambled back to the road. They stopped once, turned, pointed at him and swiped their fingers across their throats.

Raymond's mother pulled him inside the house and shut the door.

'What on earth was all that about?'

Raymond tried to speak but the words caught in his throat; the adrenalin that had kept him running abandoned him and he felt tears forming in the corner of his eyes.

'It's nothing, Mum. They're from the social.'

'They were talking about Ernest as well though, weren't they? I heard them.'

'Honestly, Mum, it's nothing. I got to go now. I need to give my flowers some water.'

'You never had trouble like this before you met him, Ray. It's not healthy. You need to find friends of your own age.'

Raymond turned to face his mum, his anger swelling. 'He's my friend, Mum,' he said, his voice rising with indignation. 'It doesn't matter how old he is. If it weren't for him they'd have beaten me up at the social. And, anyway, I'm going round his at eleven o'clock tomorrow night. I don't care what anyone says.'

Raymond's mum looked sharply at him.

'*What?* Don't be ridiculous. You can't go round someone's house at nearly midnight. For goodness' sake Ray, what's got into you? What're you going to do there anyway, and for one thing how will you get there?'

'Please, Mum. Ernest said it was his favourite night of the year; it's meteors or something – it begins with a P.'

Raymond's mum was silent for a moment. Then she smiled.

'The Perseid meteor shower?' she asked.

Raymond looked quizzically at his mum. 'Yes, that's right. How do you know?'

She laughed. 'Ray, one day you'll realise there's more to my life than looking after you and your dad. When I was your age, I spent hours staring at the stars with a small telescope my grandfather bought me one Christmas. It was my favourite thing to do.' She rubbed her arm, smiling.

'You never said.' An idea flashed before him. 'Mum! You could watch it with us. We could invite Ernest round here.'

His mum shook her head. 'Ray, what am I going to do with you?' She stood looking at him, gently holding his gaze. 'You know, when you were a little boy the tiniest of things would delight you. Catching a falling leaf before it touched the ground, Dougal the dog, finding a silver sixpence in a Christmas pudding ... oh Christmas ... Christmas ...' Her eyes began to close and Raymond smiled. 'Oh, goodness.' She sighed and waved her hands towards him. 'I give up. Go on then – phone him, but God knows what your dad will say.'

'*Yes!*' Raymond said. 'Thanks, Mum.' And he hurried to the phone.

As he dialled the numbers and listened to the whirring clicks in the earpiece, he looked out of the window. Swaying in the breeze were his sunflowers and, despite the long shadows of late afternoon, they looked greener and healthier than ever before. Raymond was sure they'd grown since this morning; large buds were now forming.

As the phone connected and began to ring, he couldn't help but grin to himself, the earlier trauma now a distant memory.

CHAPTER SIXTEEN

The Perseid Meteor Shower

It was nearly quarter past eleven.

Raymond and his mum sat quietly in the kitchen and sipped coffee. Small fluorescent lights under the wall cupboards illuminated the worktops, giving the room an expensive but cosy feel. Raymond knew his parents only used these if a special guest was coming and he smiled and hummed to himself.

The doorbell rang.

'It's him,' said Raymond, banging his cup on to the table so hard that some of the liquid slopped out. He leapt to his feet and ran to the door.

'Careful,' his mother called after him.

After a mumbled conversation in the hallway, Raymond returned to the kitchen with Ernest, who was suitably attired in a white overcoat.

'Good evening, Mrs Mann.' Ernest smiled cautiously. 'We weren't really introduced last time we met, were we? I'm

Ernest Gardiner, but please call me Ernie.' Ernest extended his hand. Raymond's mum hesitated for a moment before reaching forward and shaking it, all the while searching the older man's eyes.

'Nice to meet you. I'm June,' she said.

'Will Mr Mann be joining us tonight?' Ernest enquired.

'Um, no ... no. He has work tomorrow so he needs an early night. It's a five thirty start in the morning for him.'

'Good gracious, that is early. I can understand him wanting to get off to bed. We'll have to be quiet. Look, I've brought us some soup.' Ernest opened his carrier bag and placed two large flasks on the kitchen table. 'Hope you like tomato.'

'Oh, yes and Mum has put baked potatoes in the oven. Come on, let's go outside,' said Raymond excitedly.

His mum looked at Raymond and shook her head, smiling all the while.

'Put your coat on, Ray. It's cold out there tonight.'

'Oh Mum!' Raymond huffed and ran up the stairs to his bedroom.

* * *

June smiled at Ernest and led the way outside. Three deck chairs were already positioned in the garden, and Raymond had placed half a dozen lanterns around them. Several swayed on hooks while others stood on the grass. The golden candlelight lit the lawn, washing away the shadows and turning the garden into a magical grotto, the stars like silver glow worms twinkling in the darkness.

'Thank you so much for inviting me round,' said Ernest. 'I've spent this night by myself the last few years. My wife Violet and I would always make this a special evening – she knew how much I enjoyed it.'

'Your wife?' said June.

'Yes, we were married for fifty years. Violet died three years ago. I've been so lonely ever since. But, I have to say; your son has really brightened up my days. He's been wonderful.'

June felt pride bubbling inside – a warm chocolate cosiness that made her stomach tingle. She beamed at Ernest.

'Thank you for spending time with Raymond,' she said. 'I know we got off on the wrong foot. He's not the easiest person to get along with. He's always been, well,' – she clasped her hands together — 'a little different to his friends.' The words came out in a rush.

Ernest smiled. 'Different is all right; he just seems a little shy to me. I was like that when I was his age. I wouldn't say boo to a goose but that's changed now.' Ernest laughed. 'It's certainly not all one-way. Raymond's made me look forward to getting up in the morning. I thought those days had gone.'

The back door opened and Raymond appeared in a black duffel coat. He sank into a deckchair next to his mother and looked up at the dark sky while rubbing his hands together.

'I do hope this won't be disappointing,' said Ernest. 'It's so cloudy tonight.'

'No, look, I'm sure I saw one,' Raymond replied, excitement in his voice.

'Let me get the soup and potatoes; they should be ready now. Don't start without me,' said June, laughing at her joke as she walked back to the kitchen.

'Can I help?' called Ernest, but she'd already closed the door behind her.

* * *

Ernest and Raymond sat in the deckchairs and breathed the night air. Only the hum of traffic mingled with the sound of crickets could be heard. They sat in easy silence, looking skywards, but only static stars met their gaze.

'Oh, goodness, I'm sure it's going to be too cloudy tonight,' said Ernest. Then a white line shot across the sky. 'Did you see that?'

Raymond was already standing. 'Mum, Mum, quick it's happening,' he shouted.

June came out carrying a tray overflowing with potatoes, crisps, chocolate, mugs and Ernest's flasks of soup.

'Shhh, you'll wake the whole neighbourhood,' she said in an exaggerated whisper. She sat down in the empty deckchair, distributed the mugs and filled them with the hot tomato soup. Steam from the flasks caught in the flickering light of the lanterns and rose into the dark night sky.

From the kitchen a clock faintly chimed in the midnight hour.

June handed round the potatoes. Butter oozed out from the silver foil and on to the plates. Ernest took a large bite of his. The heat surprised him and he jerked, covering his open mouth with his hand as he breathed in and out.

'I'm so sorry – pardon me,' he said, but Raymond and June laughed and Ernest joined in.

Then, as if the heavens had been waiting for the right moment, a streak of white flashed across the sky, followed by another, then another. Some lasted only seconds – white rapiers incising the darkness – while others moved majestically across the sky, golden cloaks billowing from their royal charges. Slowly the panorama built into a blur of whooshing lines crisscrossing the darkness.

'I can't believe it,' said Ernest, his eyes wide with wonder. 'It looked so cloudy.'

'Oh, goodness,' said June, words seemingly almost beyond her. She breathed again and quickly smiled, as though to hide her embarrassment. Raymond saw her shiver and tears well in her eyes. 'It's so beautiful,' she said in barely a whisper. Her hand moved to Raymond's and rested gently on top.

Raymond, acutely aware of the touch, looked over at his mum. Despite every nerve willing him to pull his hand away, he did not. In that moment he glimpsed the woman, and for the first time understood her. In the flickering light he saw the small girl, watching in wonder at the stars, with her tiny telescope. Then the young woman, probably not much older than he was now, about to get married, with her hopes and fears, disappointments and dreams ... her whole life stretching ahead of her.

In that moment, he felt the spark of her love as it shot across the sky with comets' tails and fell into his grateful hands.

Joyous warmth overwhelmed him and he breathed

deeply. He was part of the world and so loved, but he also felt free and able to follow his own path. One day he too would have to let go and pass his unending love to another pair of tiny hands that he'd set fair upon the earth.

He looked up at the sky and smiled. And for the first time since he was a small child cradled in his parent's arms, he felt at ease.

'Once, a friend of mine said there was so much beauty in the world,' said Ernest. 'A sky full of stars. I think we've gone one better – a sky full of shooting stars.'

The sky erupted in a silver symphony of light.

Three faces flashed white. Laughter and gasps of awe floated upwards to weave with the stars and to one day return as the breeze, washing over closed eyes on a summer's day.

Above them in the bedroom, Raymond's dad watched through the window.

He was smiling.

CHAPTER SEVENTEEN
The Seagull

The summer seemed to pass in the blink of an eye. In previous years, Raymond had hidden in his room, only venturing out to tend the garden, but this summer his face and arms displayed the glow of long days spent in the sunshine. Whenever he glimpsed himself in the mirror, his darker complexion surprised him. He felt fit and healthy; each morning seemed to bring something new to look forward to.

After the Perseid meteor shower, Raymond's parents had warmed to Ernest and, to Raymond's amazement, agreed they could spend more time together, even plan a holiday. From that moment on, the two had become inseparable.

Now the summer was almost over and Raymond dozed as the countryside drifted by. They'd left Dorset that morning but home was still four hours away. A political discussion crackling on the car radio captivated

Ernest but Raymond had no interest. Instead, he thought about the past six weeks, which had begun in London and ended that morning in Weymouth. The weather had been glorious throughout and beautiful blue skies provided a perfect backdrop to their days.

A week after the meteor display, they'd met at The Salt Shaker. Keith, the owner, had joined them as they pulled the two round tables together and spread out their maps. Raymond was offered chilli con carne in a white polystyrene cup and the two older men had laughed as he refused to try it, despite their encouragement and proffered plastic spoon.

Keith and Ernest had debated over whether to head north or south – the Lake District or Dorset – but Ernest had won the day.

Raymond found it hard to believe – the days of planning seemed like yesterday but now they were driving home …

* * *

London was a revelation as the grandeur of the city replaced the grimy graffiti-clad walls of Liverpool Street station. The huge brick buildings, the white marble statues and the thronging crowds of tourists overwhelmed Raymond, and he turned on the spot, breathing in the sights and sounds.

Ernest led the way to Westminster Abbey and Raymond tingled as he looked up at the vaulted roof and dazzling stained glass. They walked along the darkened aisles and into the South Transept until they stood quietly in Poets' Corner, looking at the engraved memorials.

'This is what I wanted to show you,' said Ernest smiling. 'Look at all these names: Chaucer, Dickens, Wordsworth, Austen and the Brontë's. Maybe one day Raymond, in a very long time, of course,' – he chuckled – 'if you keep up your writing and want to do it more than anything else in the world, they'll be honouring you.' He poked a friendly finger at Raymond's sternum.

'Get out of it,' said Raymond, laughing but nevertheless moved by Ernest's words and his faith in the future. He felt warm and was sure others must be able to see him illuminated in the gloom.

Ernest pointed towards a marble plaque. Around the outer edge, carved in red, were the words *My subject is war, and the pity of war. The poetry is in the pity.* Within the inscription was a column of sixteen names, listed in alphabetical order. The eleventh was Wilfred Owen.

Raymond stared at the plaque and imagined the men in the mud and the debris, frightened and homesick. He found it hard to understand how Ernest had coped. He'd been so young, little more than a boy; it was all so difficult to comprehend. There in the dark, he felt a surge of gratitude to all those young soldiers who'd never returned home. He looked at Ernest, who stared hard at the wall, swallowing.

Together they stood quietly, then Raymond took Ernest's arm and led him out into the sunshine.

After the visit to London, they went to the theatre and the cinema and spent lazy days sitting in the garden, talking about the war, Ernest's life and Raymond's dreams. Raymond rode home in the late-afternoon stillness, the bus empty, each journey less fraught than the last.

His dad returned home from work each evening and they sat together in the kitchen, drinking tea, while his mum cooked dinner. They talked about music and sport, but most of all about Ernest – his life, and his days in Bailleul. It was the first time Raymond could remember having a grown-up conversation with his dad and he relished those evenings, going to bed happy and content, his prayers short and thankful.

Ernest would also visit Raymond's house to tend the sunflowers – feeding them, removing dead leaves and straitening their stems. The flowers were growing taller all the time, but the green buds stubbornly refused to open.

Each day, glorious as it was, only seemed a prelude to the final part of the holiday – the trip to Dorset – and Raymond counted the hours until their departure.

They spent the first part of their break at a holiday camp in the small village of Osmington Bay, a few miles outside Weymouth.

On arrival, Ernest followed a white, hand-painted wooden sign directing them up a winding lane to the camp. The road was lined on either side by green fields stretching endlessly into the distance. They drove slowly, admiring the scenery but mindful of vehicles coming the other way. After a few hundred yards they turned a final corner and reached the brow of a hill.

The sea and sky filled the horizon. It was as though they were floating in the clouds high above the ocean, and

Raymond sucked in a shallow breath. The road curved downwards towards the holiday camp but Raymond continued to look outwards towards the sea, shielding his eyes from the diamond pinpricks that burst through the wisps of white.

The camp was full of laughter, good food and cabaret. A team of gregarious entertainers worked tirelessly to cheer their guests and Raymond admired their effortless ability to socialise easily with everyone they met.

Each morning, the bluest of skies welcomed them back to the world and gradually they found a quiet routine. On waking they would wrap up against the early-morning chill and take turns walking to the small gift shop to buy newspapers and wonderful sweet tea. Then they would hike over fields to a cliff top, where they'd stand in awe, looking down at the sand and sea hundreds of feet below.

As the morning melted into the afternoon, lunch in a local pub would be the priority. The Pirates Inn became their favourite. They sat outside on the wooden benches, enjoying a basket meal and feeling the sun on their browning faces. The pub was beamed and dark with low ceilings, and had been the home to the leader of a notorious gang of smugglers during the eighteenth and nineteenth centuries. The tales of pirates and contraband intrigued Raymond and a childhood memory of his dad telling him stories of knights and princesses, honour and adventure reminded him warmly of home and his family.

A few days later, they moved to a tired, but comfortable bed-and-breakfast in the heart of Weymouth. The tiny, elderly woman who ran it darted about with dusters and cleaning products at a speed that belied her age. Despite her size she had a formidable presence, a booming voice and a set of rules that no one dared break, the strangest of which was no red wine in the bedroom. Much to Raymond's amusement, at every opportunity, Ernest would close his eyes, put the back of his hand to his forehead and declare his need for a glass of red, despite never normally drinking it.

The final morning's breakfast was an enormous fry-up. Sausages and bacon overlapped the edge of the plate, each cooked to a perfect salty crispness. The egg was the deepest of yellows and solid the way Raymond liked it. It was a huge meal especially for Raymond, who usually only ate cornflakes, and just when he felt fit to burst, the landlady dropped a large rack of toast between them.

'I think she toasted that by breathing on it,' whispered Ernest as he mimicked a dragon.

Raymond laughed but quickly fell silent when he saw the landlady's small hawk-like eyes focus on his.

After breakfast they got their bags and waited at the bus stop outside the entrance. A light-green, bull-nosed double-decker trundled up to the stop. Despite the time of year, it was strangely empty and the two men sat upstairs alone.

The bus meandered through the narrow Weymouth streets, up the steepest of hills and out into the countryside. Raymond excitedly pointed out a large white horse and rider carved into the green hillside.

'That's George the Third. He often visited the town,' said Ernest.

They sat in silence then, shoulders pressed together, moving to the slow rhythm of the bus. They soaked up the views, trying to memorise the sky and the sea and the cliffs, building a squirrel's store of memories to warm them in winter.

As the countryside gave way to villages, Ernest noticed Raymond staring at the bell. He reached across and pushed it making Raymond jerk backwards.

'What are you doing?'

'Nothing,' said Ernest. 'I just felt like pushing it.'

The bus slowed and stopped.

'What are we going to do now?' Raymond whispered, looking around in embarrassed panic. Ernest just shrugged and smiled.

'Is this your stop?' the conductor called up the stairs gruffly.

'So sorry,' said Ernest politely. 'I'm mistaken – it's further on.'

Raymond shook his head, eyes wide in astonishment. The bus moved off again.

'You once told me you had trouble getting off buses,' whispered Ernest. 'Push it.'

'No.'

'Go on, do it.'

'No!' Raymond's hands formed a barrier in front of him.

'What's the worst that can happen?' said Ernest. 'Push it – it's a bell.'

Raymond rested his hand on the silver rail and edged towards the red circle, staring at it. Then, as if the heaviest of burdens had flown into the blue sky, he shrugged, smiled and pushed. Ernest did the same several more times.

The conductor raced up the stairs, breathing heavily.

'Can't you read? Just push once,' he said angrily.

'So sorry, Inspector,' said Ernest.

Laughter burst from Raymond's lips in a joyous, champagne explosion.

'Right, that's it. You two off ... now,' shouted the conductor. 'And for Christ's sake, grow up.'

Raymond and Ernest edged past the conductor and half-walked, half-fell down the stairs. At the bottom, Ernest looked into the cab at the furious driver and pushed the button again. Raymond followed suit several times. *Ding, ding, ding, ding.* The sound echoed through the empty bus.

'Grow up, you bloody idiots,' shouted the driver as the two jumped off the platform and skipped down the road.

'What did I tell you?' said Ernest. 'It was a bell. It was fun! And what's the worst that could've happened? You mustn't worry so much.'

'I know,' said Raymond, smiling. 'Ernest, we're skipping.'

Ernest grinned. 'I know.'

* * *

They waited at the next stop in silence until another bus arrived and took them to Lulworth Cove.

It was mid-afternoon and the throngs of tourists were making plans to leave although the sun was still high in the sky.

Ernest and Raymond walked through the car park and down to the sandy bay sheltered on three sides by white cliffs. They lay down on the pebble beach near the rocks and watched the world – there were families splashing in the sea, building sandcastles and eating ice creams. They hugged, jumped, ran and squealed. Their laughter fused with the sound of the sea and the chatter of seagulls, to form a perfect backdrop.

Raymond closed his eyes and listened.

He felt the breeze gently cooling his face and imagined being anywhere in the world and this same simple scene playing out over and over throughout time.

He prayed it would always be so.

'One hundred prayers, Lord,' he muttered, then, with a start, realised he'd spoken out loud. But Ernest only turned his head and smiled.

As if reading Raymond's thoughts, he said sadly, 'Oh, Raymond, all the things we do to each other in the world. It's still so beautiful. Why oh why can't we all get along? There's got to be a better way, hasn't there? All the food we have in Europe and nothing in Africa; the troubles in Ireland. I want everyone to share this perfect moment.'

Raymond turned and touched the older man's arm. Ernest smiled.

'I'm sorry to be sad,' he said. 'It's just so wonderful. I'm a stupid old codger. Come on – I'll show you something.'

Raymond followed Ernest out of the cove. They walked back through the emptying car park and made their way towards a steep hill in the distance. The path was narrow and they strolled in single file, passing other walkers on their way back down. Everyone seemed to be in a happy mood and they exchanged frequent pleasantries as they climbed.

'Afternoon.'

'Hello.'

'Lovely day.'

To their left, the sea swelled gently, tiny flecks of white riding the waves then disappearing into the dark blue. Above them, seagulls hovered, slightly tilting their wings to get the best of the thermal currents.

A younger bird, snowy white with slate-grey wings, flew alongside the two men, flapping, cawing and hoping, Raymond thought, for some titbits. But the bird just seemed to enjoy the quickening breeze and soared up and down at speed, as if showing off its skills. Then it glided close to them and looked directly into Raymond's smiling eyes. For the briefest of moments, two hearts rejoiced at the simple pleasure of being alive.

It was a difficult climb; Ernest was breathing heavily, silver drops of perspiration beading his forehead.

'You okay?' Raymond asked.

'I'm fine,' said Ernest, catching his breath. 'I was here only a few years ago and hadn't realised just how old I'd become in the meantime.'

They reached the summit. The path ahead wound downwards over some narrow steps.

'This is what I wanted you to see,' said Ernest, and he pointed towards a large dark rock formation rising from the sea. 'That's Durdle Door.'

But Raymond had already seen it and was looking

across at the rocky promontory, mesmerised by the waves washing against the large natural arch formed in the limestone. Far below, several canoeists were paddling through the archway and the last few tourists were making the most of the surf.

'I love it here,' said Ernest. 'I've been so many times with Violet. The weather has always been good. It's such a happy place; today it's perfect again.'

Raymond looked at Ernest, trying desperately to see beyond the skin and bone, to feel the essence of this kind and gentle man who'd shown him how to be happy. He wished with all his heart to have shared Ernest's memories, to be part of his history, but as he stood on the hill, the sun low in the sky, he knew that could never be. So, with a determined sigh, he quietly vowed to make his own history and to share it with someone else at this same spot.

He closed his eyes and gently moved his head, breathing deeply as the wind cooled his face and ruffled his hair. There was nothing more to do or say that would add to the moment so he walked down the path towards the shore, leaving Ernest to his memories.

Raymond sat on the beach and waited for his friend to join him. The older man struggled on the steep steps; the stiffness in his joints clear and he grasped the rusty handrail. When he reached the bottom, he gave a small reassuring wave, ambled over to Raymond and lowered himself awkwardly on to the pebbly beach.

They sat in silence, looking out over the sea towards the horizon. The sun was even lower and the shadows had lengthened, dark now against the yellow sand. Most of the sightseers had packed up and left for the day, leaving only those stubborn enough to wring the most from the last remnants of the afternoon. There was a quiet peacefulness, and a gentle warmth replaced the earlier heat.

'This is my favourite time of the day,' said Ernest. 'Violet and I used to go to Walton – we had a lovely little beach hut on the prom. We'd sit and watch the crowds leaving; then it would just be us and the seagulls calling overhead. Violet would always reach over and find my fingers; she'd rest her hand in my lap, our shoulders touching ... I miss that.'

Ernest looked away from Raymond, feigning interest in the long stretch of beach but Raymond could see his friend's sadness.

'Come on,' he said, standing quickly.

Without looking back, Raymond jogged to the sea. Ernest turned and watched, propping himself up on one elbow and shielding his eyes from the sun with his free hand. Raymond reached the water's edge, hesitated for a moment as the bubbling foam washed over his trainers, and then, without further thought, walked into the water fully clothed.

The cold sea took his breath away as the waves lapped against his knees and then his thighs.

The water was already up to Raymond's waist before Ernest struggled to his feet and put his hands on his hips.

'What are you doing?' he called, trying not to smile.

Raymond jumped up and down and laughed, his arms outstretched. He beckoned Ernest to join him but Ernest shook his head.

'You'll be frozen! We have to get back to the hotel. You're mad!'

'Come on,' said Raymond, laughing. 'You only live once.'

Ernest looked around. There were still several families dotted about on the beach and Raymond's actions had drawn their attention. Ernest took a deep breath and hobbled slowly over the stones towards the sea. He didn't stop when he reached the water and appeared oblivious to the cold as he wandered into the waves and stood, half-submerged, next to Raymond.

'Happy now?' he said, tilting his head to one side.

'Not … quite … yet,' said Raymond, and he splashed Ernest. The tiny droplets of water seemed to hang in the air as the sun refracted through them.

'Why you—' said Ernest surprised. 'Now you're going to get a nuclear retaliation.' Ernest sent huge sprays of water over Raymond, not stopping even when he surrendered and held his hands to cover his face.

'There, you can't mess with a super power,' said Ernest, grinning. Raymond took his chance, grabbing Ernest around the neck and pulling him into the sea.

Drenched and choking, they stood and wiped the water from their eyes. Once the stinging salt had cleared and they could see each other again, neither could stop the splutters of laughter that filled the air. They linked arms and walked back to the sand.

Raymond waved at the people on the beach, calling them over, but they shook their heads and walked away as if certain they were witnessing the after-effects of a drunken afternoon in Weymouth.

The two men flopped down on to the sand and lay outstretched, looking up at the blue sky, feeling the sea breeze, on their wet clothes. Ernest was breathing heavily but it didn't stop his smile as the sun gently warmed him.

'Thank you for sharing such a perfect day,' he said quietly.

Raymond laughed. 'Don't be daft, Granddad.'

'Why, you young whippersnapper, how you've changed,' replied Ernest, but he looked at Raymond and felt a pride so strong that it burned inside of him, and he was sure no father could have been happier.

* * *

'Raymond, Raymond. Wake up. We're here,' said Ernest, nudging him.

Raymond opened his eyes. He'd been sleeping and wondered where those four hours had gone. He smiled and couldn't remember a time since he was tiny when he'd been happier.

'Thanks, Ernest,' he said.

'What for?'

'Just ... just for everything. It's been a great summer.'

'Yes,' said Ernest, laughing. 'It has, hasn't it? Tell you what, tonight I'll teach you how to fly. Well, the closest you can get to it without your feet leaving the ground. Meet me at The Quiet Life at nine. You know, the pub on the hill near my house. We need three pints before closing. Reckon you can manage that?'

CHAPTER EIGHTEEN

Learning to Fly

The Quiet Life was a proper British pub – two bars, the public and saloon, and a tiny off-licence where every night an elderly man leant against the scarred green counter. He would wobble along the road on his bicycle, arrive at opening time, and remain until last orders, making his slowly sipped pint last the whole evening. A white terrier sat by his feet and was rewarded for its patience with a packet of ready salted crisps, which, unlike the beer, lasted only seconds.

The saloon bar was warm and welcoming. Plush salmon-coloured banquettes lined the walls and small wooden tables took up the space in the middle, their chairs pointing towards a central chimney and an unlit fire.

A young barmaid chatted happily to the elderly patrons while Henry, the craggy landlord, hovered in the background, adjusting the drip trays, straightening the bar towels and ensuring everything ran smoothly. His large moustache often displayed white bubbles of froth acquired from a surreptitious sip of beer, bought by a customer wishing to gain favour. On the odd occasion when he served behind the bar, he would tilt his head to one side and close an eye in an act of scientific concentration as he pulled the pump slowly towards him, ensuring the perfect pint. Less kind patrons often commented that he was judging the volume of beer to the nth degree, never exceeding the white measurement line. Unbeknown to Henry, some younger customers would mimic his beer-pulling technique, much to the merriment of the pub.

Ernest and Raymond sat carefree and happy in the corner. The alcohol had done its work, and they were perched on the precipice of gay abandon but not quite ready to dive into drunkenness. An empty beer mug and pint glass sat on the table in front of them. A red Embassy ashtray held down a pile of flattened crisp packets and a lacy haze of smoke smudged the air. The sound of pool balls clacking and the odd groan or cheer could be heard from the public bar.

'Last orders,' the landlord shouted above the dull hubbub.

'You want another?' asked Raymond.

'No thanks,' replied Ernest. 'I've done this many times before. We need that early glow of drunkenness but we also need to be able to run.' He chuckled.

'Ernest! What *are* we going to do? *Tell me!*'

'All will be revealed. Let's go.'

* * *

Ernest and Raymond stood at the top of the gently sloping hill, their heads close together in whispered conversation. Ernest wore his white overcoat buttoned tightly to the neck; in contrast, Raymond's black duffel flapped open.

The anticipation was electric, and their breath came in bursts as their pulses quickened. It began to rain.

Raymond lifted his head and let the drops fall into his eyes and into his open mouth, catching them on his tongue. He turned on the spot with his face to the sky watching Ernest share his joy.

Ernest raised his arms, Christ-like, palms upwards catching the rain.

'Are you ready?' he whispered. 'It's the closest you'll get to flying without leaving the ground.'

'Show me,' said Raymond, his voice barely audible.

Ernest lowered his arms, reached into his coat pocket and pulled out a small round object. It was a French franc, battered and brown, its long history evident in the smoothness of its surface. He caressed it between his thumb and forefinger. After so many years the movement of his circling thumb was as natural as blinking.

'Follow it down the hill. Go as quickly as your legs will take you. Leap whenever you can and don't stop even if you overtake it.'

Raymond looked down the slope and adjusted his position, imitating a runner about to start a race. Ernest swung his arm back and smoothly sent the coin rolling and bouncing down the hill.

For a second, Raymond rocked back on his heels, surprised by the strength of Ernest's throw, and then he leapt after the coin. He'd never been athletic and this was evident in his ungainly run and flailing arms as he plummeted down the slope.

He gained speed, the incline of the hill assisting his momentum. And now his legs could barely keep up with him – sometimes it seemed as if his feet missed the ground completely. The breeze and the sound of his footsteps pounding the pavement were all he could hear. Then he leapt, arms outstretched, and everything was quiet for the briefest of moments. He landed lightly and continued to run faster and faster. The street lights, the stars and the pavement merged into a mist-filled swirl.

Eyes closed, mouth open, gasping with joy, he ran and leapt, overtaking the franc that had now fallen on its side.

And then it was over.

Raymond was at the bottom of the hill and he jogged to a halt. He bent, put his hands on his knees and panted heavily. As his breath returned, he straightened, raised his arms to the stars and jumped, laughing and whooping.

Ernest walked down the hill towards the franc. Lost in thought, he bent slowly to pick it up, passed it between his fingers and squeezed it in his hands.

'Come on. You do it. You must – please, you must!' Raymond shouted up the slope, his voice cutting through the silence.

'I can't. I'm past all that. How did it feel?' he said.

'Like I was the wind! Please do it.'

Smiling, Ernest looked at the coin and once more sent it rolling down the hill. He ran after it, stuttering on stiff legs until his momentum, fuelled by the hill and gravity, began to increase and in an act of grace and wonder, he leapt.

Raymond stood open-mouthed as he watched his friend rise into the air; saw him freeze-framed in flight, a huge smile on his face, his arms flung forward, legs poised like a long jumper's.

In an instant, the world spun back to grey reality as Ernest's feet returned to the earth and his legs buckled under his weight. Arms outstretched, he tottered forward and crumpled on to his open hands and bent knees.

He lay motionless, face down, his white coat rising and falling with each heavy breath.

'Ernest!' Raymond shouted, and ran up the hill.

Ernest slowly rolled over and sat up, his head resting on his knees. Raymond skidded to a halt in front of him.

'Ernest! Ernest, are you all right?'

'I'm fine,' he replied, brushing the dirt from his trousers. 'It's just my pride. Thank goodness it's dark.' He laughed, then winced.

Raymond lifted Ernest to his feet and helped him over the road to the grass verge. Ernest gingerly sat down on a plastic grit bin and looked at his palms; they were bleeding.

'What a foolish old man I am,' he said. 'Trouble is, I don't feel old. I wanted to fly like you. Not that long ago I could do it.' He looked down at his torn trousers; a glistening red stain had formed on each knee. 'When we met, you seemed scared of living. Well, you know what?' He sighed. 'I'm scared of dying. I just keep thinking of all the wonderful things that are going to happen and how I'll miss them all.'

They sat in silence while Ernest's breathing returned to normal. It was still raining and the two men looked a forlorn sight, perched on the yellow bin sagging under their weight.

Raymond moved closer and the bin dipped a little more.

'All my so-called friends at school had a party once,' he said. 'A reunion. The only thing was they forgot, or … or … probably didn't want to invite me. But … I didn't miss going because I didn't know it had happened. It was only a long time afterwards when somebody told me about it that I felt bad and wished I'd been there. Before then, I was absolutely fine.'

The silence continued. Then Ernest grinned and began to laugh, louder and louder, holding his ribs and grimacing.

'You're right, you're so right; how can I miss things I don't even know will happen? What I'll miss are my memories. That's it. It's my *memories* I'll miss and I've already had those. They've been so wonderful, but I can't have them again, can I? Oh, Raymond, why didn't I think of that?' Ernest put his arm around Raymond's shoulder. 'Goddamn it, Raymond. How did you get to be so clever?'

Raymond looked through the drizzle and found Ernest's smiling eyes.

'I had the best teacher,' he said quietly.

'It's been an honour, my friend,' said Ernest, returning Raymond's gaze.

'Don't talk of sad things; I've learnt to fly. Come on – let's get you home, then you can order me a taxi.'

Ernest struggled to his feet, took a single step and stumbled. Raymond moved closer and held him tightly around the waist. He lifted Ernest's arm and wrapped it around his neck and the two began a slow, staccato walk home.

'Wait, hang on – stop a minute,' said Ernest, and they paused. He reached into his pocket. 'You have this. Please look after it – I hope it'll bring as much luck and joy to your life as it has to mine. Mira gave it to me.'

Ernest handed Raymond the old French franc.

'Thanks, Ernest, but are you sure? It must mean so much to you.'

'I'm sure,' said Ernest. 'Now home, James!'

'James?'

'It's just a—'

'I know.'

They walked up the hill towards the moonlight and the threads of white clouds. The drizzle wet their faces and made their clothes stick uncomfortably to their arms and legs. But rather than dampening Ernest's spirits, it seemed to lift him, and he couldn't stop himself from smiling as Raymond tenderly supported him, a wounded soldier returning from a last battle.

CHAPTER NINETEEN

The Book Club

Raymond was up early – unusual for the weekend. Several days had passed since he'd flown down the hill, but the memory still blazed hot within him. He'd been tending his sunflowers every day, willing them to bloom, but the enlarging buds remained stubbornly closed.

This morning was no different and he weeded around the roots, absentmindedly removing the curled brown leaves. The early-morning sun had yet to dispel the chill in the air; autumn would soon be upon them and end any hope of seeing his sunflowers bloom.

He felt a sharp sting on his back and reached behind, thinking a bee had become trapped in his jumper. Then a stone whizzed past his head and landed with a puff of dust in the flowerbed.

'Hello, Mr Bender.' One of the skinheads leant over the wall. 'Any news about your old poofter friend?'

Raymond stood. 'Just leave me alone. I haven't done anything to you.'

'No, but we'll make do with you if we can't find the old poof. What're you doing anyway, you fucking homo? Looking after your pussy flowers?'

The skinhead lunged forward. Raymond backed away and stumbled over his trowel.

The yob sniggered, a mean cold laugh. 'I got a fucking football match otherwise I'd love to stay and play, but I'll be back.' And he blew Raymond a kiss before continuing down the road.

Raymond put his tools away and walked to the house. He sat down at the kitchen table, shaky and uncomfortable. His mum and dad were already eating toast and drinking coffee, his dad engrossed in a book.

'You were late last night, Ray,' his mum said. 'Who were you talking to outside just now?'

'Oh, nobody. Just someone from the social.' His pounding heart returned to normal, soothed by the warmth of the kitchen and his mother's voice. 'I went to the pub last night with Andy – you know, the boy I used to be friends with at school. I saw him yesterday afternoon and he said it would be good to catch up. It was great. We'll probably do it again.'

The success of the evening had surprised Raymond; he'd not been looking forward to it, but their shared school history had given them plenty to talk about. He'd grown in confidence, even making Andy laugh on several occasions, and he walked home feeling pleased with himself, the alcohol enhancing his happiness.

His mum got up to fill the kettle and get some bread for the toaster.

'I can do that, Mum. You sit down.' Raymond pushed his chair aside and moved to the bread bin. It creaked open to reveal a large white loaf.

Raymond's dad looked up from his book and smiled. 'Morning, Ray. Where did you say Ernest was during the war?'

'Hello. Umm, it was something like Ballyor. What're you reading, Dad?'

'It's a book about the First World War. I got it from the club – it was only two bob, well, ten pence. You wouldn't believe what those soldiers went through; they were only youngsters. Some were even shot for desertion. It was terrible … terrible, the conditions … goodness me.'

'I know. I've told you that, Dad. Ernest was only seventeen.'

'Seventeen …' His dad flicked through the pages. 'Ah, here it is. I thought I'd seen it somewhere.' He adjusted his glasses and began to read. 'On the 14th of October 1914, the 19th Brigade occupied Bailleul. It became an important railhead, air depot and hospital centre.' He glanced up from the book to look at Raymond, who sat, fascinated. 'It goes on to say that the Australians used it as a casualty clearing station and it was headquarters to the British Army until July 1917, when the Germans severely bombed the town. It fell into German hands after the Battle of Bailleul in April 1918. The British recaptured it in August 1918.'

Raymond stood up and walked behind his dad.

'Listen to this,' continued his dad. 'Only ruins of the town remained. Ninety-eight per cent of it was destroyed.

At one time they were just going to leave it as a reminder of the war, rather than rebuilding.'

Raymond frowned and moved his head closer, almost touching his dad's. He ran his finger along the lines his father had read.

'Hang on. That can't be right,' he said. 'It must be a different place. Ernest told me he'd spent the last year of the war there, and it was peaceful. Can I see?'

His dad passed Raymond the book.

'That's funny. I'm sure that's the place Ernest said. I'll ask him. Thanks, Dad.'

Raymond sat down and ate his toast, staring into the distance as he tried to remember Ernest's words.

'You all right, Ray?' said his mum.

'Yes, I'm fine, I'm … I'm going to see Ernest. I'll see you later.'

Raymond forced the last piece of toast into his already full mouth, gulped some coffee and went up to his bedroom.

* * *

The bus trip was uneventful, and Raymond confidently rang the bell for his stop and departed the bus, a smile on his face.

Reaching Ernest's house, his eyes were once more drawn to the dozen large sunflowers that lined the wall, each of them standing tall, their large yellow flowers pointing skywards, determined to catch every drop of sunlight.

Ernest opened the door.

'I saw you coming,' he said, smiling. 'Cup of tea?'

He led the way into the lounge, limping badly. The large dark bruise on his forehead shocked Raymond.

'What have you been up to? I haven't seen you for a few days.'

'Oh, nothing much. I've been looking after my garden. The sunflowers are still growing but I think it's too late for them to bloom now. Yours are great. Are you okay? How's your leg?'

Ernest shrugged. 'Oh, I'm fine, and it's all right, thanks. Give your sunflowers a chance – there's still a couple of weeks of summer, they might be late developers.' He smiled.

'I went to the pub, too, with a friend from school, which was nice, and … and I've been trying to write some poems. I might even try a story next.' He looked away, embarrassed.

'My goodness, you have been busy. Remember your author's name?'

'Oh, yes, my mum's maiden name and, er—'

'Your first pet's name.'

'I remember,' said Raymond, laughing. 'It's Dougal Hyland.'

'That's it. Come on then, Dougal. Let me hear what you've done.'

'No way – they're not ready yet,' said Raymond, taking a step backwards. 'Anyway, I wanted to ask you where you were at the end of the war.'

'I told you,' said Ernest. 'Bailleul.'

'That's what I thought, but my dad has a book that said the Germans almost bombed it flat in July 1917. But I remember you saying it was really peaceful.'

Ernest licked his lips and looked around the room. He sighed deeply.

'Er ... yes, it was very peaceful,' he said too quickly. 'Now let me get us that tea.'

Raymond persisted. 'Was it a different place? Did you see any bombs near you?'

Ernest seemed to stumble. He reached for his armchair and fell into it, then leant forward, resting his forehead in his hands.

He took a deep breath and shook his head. 'I'm so sorry, Raymond. I haven't been completely truthful with you; you're my friend and you deserve better. It's just that it was so awful. Would you like me to tell you the whole story? How it really was?'

CHAPTER TWENTY

Ernest's Story (Part Three)

1917

Ernest, Bill and Mira sat by the river. It was a beautiful July day. The sun soared high in the sky and the heat was dark and dense, making every movement a struggle.

Ernest and Bill lay bare-chested on the river bank, their feet dangling in the cool, fast-running water, hands behind their heads, cushioning the ground. The contrast between the two men was clear – Bill, muscular and brown, his experience etched in the contours of his body; Ernest, skinny and pale, still waiting to lose his wiry innocence.

Mira sat between the two, legs bent and cradled in her arms, her head on her knees. Her eyes were closed and her long hair fell over her shoulders, black as night against her white dress. Perspiration beaded her olive skin and the open neck of her unbuttoned dress fluttered in the cooling breeze.

Bill opened one eye and looked across at her.

'You been using your Sunlight soap on Ernie? He's whiter than one of your sheets.'

Mira laughed, her voice like a song, and she leaned back to look at the men beside her, supporting her weight on long, slender arms. Ernest sat up and self-consciously covered his chest, but Mira reached over and gently took his hand and smiled.

Bill raised himself on to his elbows. He shook his head and stared at Ernest, then stuck out his tongue and laughed.

They'd been living in Mira's house. The search continued for a horse that had not been spooked by the bombs, and every day that the general's photo shoot was delayed saw ever-wider smiles bloom on their faces.

It had been idyllic. The three had become inseparable. They lived in a parallel universe, far removed from the mud filled trenches and the smell of death; it had become hard to believe that another darker place existed so close by.

Their days took on a familiar pattern: breakfast at the farmhouse followed by a slow walk through the countryside to the river, where they'd sit and talk about their lives before the war.

Mira's stories of the farm intrigued the men, especially Bill, who'd never set foot outside the city. She told them about her father, how there'd always been a special bond between them, that it had often been the two of them against the world. He'd insisted, against all convention, and to the annoyance of his neighbours, that she be educated rather than marry the first farmer who asked for her hand, and she was grateful. But now she was desperately worried. Her fiancé had been killed and there'd been no news of her father.

Ernest and Bill tried to ease her fears, telling her tales of the trenches that included only the humour and none of the horror. Their eyes would meet as they told these half-truths, each word born from straight, thin lips that should have betrayed their feelings, though Mira never seemed to notice.

At lunchtime Mira would open a creaking wicker basket and spread a red tablecloth over the grass. On that she'd set yellow cheese, crispy French bread, brown pickle, so chunky that the vegetables were easily recognisable within it, and a bottle of homemade red wine that had been fermenting since before the war. Their stomachs rumbled as they waited patiently for Mira to fill their glasses and say a short prayer of thanks.

Ernest was some ten years younger than his friends and his worldly inexperience made him feel inadequate. He was in awe of Bill's ability to find the right words and to make Mira laugh, and the deep well of stories seemed never to run dry. Each meandering tale would end with his favourite saying – that everything happened for a reason. Mira and Ernest usually anticipated the conclusion of a story and would mimic Bill mercilessly amid hoots of laughter.

Despite his quietness, Mira always took Ernest's hand on their way back to the farmhouse, or wove his arm through hers as she laughed during Bill's stories. He wondered if her actions were maternal or whether she liked him, and as the days passed he felt his heart miss a beat every time he saw her. When she took his hand, his body tingled.

Ernest had never been in love.

He had never felt such joy in another's company.

Mira's laugh washed over his soul and bathed him in a warm fountain of happiness. When she gazed dreamily into the distance and nervously bounced her leg, his heart melted. He imagined holding her tightly, shielding her, keeping her safe for eternity. He'd give his life for her, of that he had no doubt.

Bill teased him relentlessly, but it mattered not; inside he was aglow and had never felt happier.

After two weeks of contented idleness, the corporal knocked on the farmhouse door.

'Come on, you two. Your luck's run out. I've found a horse.' He was jubilant, and a beaming smile spread across his face.

'Good for you,' said Bill. 'I hope you'll both be very happy.' And he shut the door in the corporal's face.

The corporal banged hard on the door. 'Stop arsing about. I've had enough trouble with the general because of you two bloody idiots. Now fall in, at the double.'

Ernest picked up his camera and handed the bag of plates to Bill. They followed the corporal back along the same route they'd taken fourteen days earlier. Ernest trudged behind the soldier and his friend, marvelling at how quickly things could change. He had been in the depths of despair, so low and weak he couldn't carry on;

now the weather was fine and he'd experienced the golden glow of first love.

'What the hell's wrong with him?' said the corporal.

'Who knows?' said Bill, shaking his head in despair.

They reached the outskirts of the town; it was overflowing with soldiers, all heading towards the square. They joined the throng and were at once immersed in the excitement and jollity. It was like a public holiday. The sun shone and the men smiled and laughed, glad of some respite from the trenches.

The corporal led them down a narrow shaded side street. Ahead, a group of soldiers blocked their path. Those at the rear darted back and forth or leaned and jumped on the shoulders of the men in front, trying to force a better view. A hubbub of voices and laughter greeted them as they neared the tightly packed group of men.

'Coming through,' shouted the corporal, but the men took no notice and continued to vie for the best vantage point. 'Out of the way,' he shouted again. 'General's orders.' And he grabbed one man by his jacket collar and pulled him aside.

'What the fuck!' snarled the soldier and raised his fists.

'These men have to see the general,' shouted the corporal. 'Help me get them through and I'll see you have a front-row spot.'

The soldier thought for a moment, realised he'd nothing to lose and ploughed into the melee.

'Emergency, out of the way,' he shouted. 'The general's waiting for these men.'

There was a dull moaning and groaning and some

momentary flashes of temper, but the path slowly cleared. Bill and Ernest followed close behind. Bill holding on to the corporal's shoulders, the bag of plates tucked close to his body. Ernest hung to Bill's waist; his head low against his friend's back. They felt like royalty battling their way through an adoring crowd.

Then, as if a storm had passed, they were free of the crowd and standing in the town square, surrounded on all sides by a mass of dull brown and green. It was an undulating wave, broken every now and again as a single soldier was pushed out of line and into the square.

Bill and Ernest looked around, shielding their eyes from the blazing midday sun. They felt vulnerable, like Christians about to be fed to the lions, the baying masses eager for blood.

In the middle of the square stood a large chestnut mare. It shook its head furiously and danced on its front legs as if the ground were too hot for its hooves. The groom tried to keep its head still but the horse whinnied and lifted him off his feet.

The general perched precariously on the saddle and grabbed the reins, pulling the mare's head backwards. The whites of the horse's eyes bulged and its ears were folded back in fear and confusion.

The general saw Bill and Ernest and beckoned them over.

'Thank God you're here. This damn horse is supposed to be as gentle as a bloody lamb,' he said, huffing. 'But I think it's going to bolt at any moment.' He shortened the reins and the horse whinnied and raised its front legs again.

The general wore his full-dress uniform, the reds bright against the wall of dull brown and green. The dazzling silver regalia sent bright arrows of sunlight into the eyes of the onlookers.

'I say, keep this goddamn thing still, can't you?' he hollered at the anxious groom.

Bill stepped forward.

'Right, Ernie, you go over there and set up your camera. I'll try to hold this horse.'

Ernest inserted the glass plates into his camera, as the hilarity of the watching soldiers grew louder and echoed around the square.

'I really don't know if this is such a good idea,' said the general, straining as he tried to control the agitated horse. 'Perhaps I could just stand and point my rifle, eh?' Ernest noticed him glance at his men, as if pondering how he might get out of the situation without losing face. 'Cameraman, *Cameraman*, what do you say?'

Ernest looked up and was about to answer, but Bill interrupted.

'No, General. Sir, this will make a wonderful shot – just think of those statues in London.'

The general sighed and puffed. 'I suppose you're right. Just get the damn thing done, will you, before this bloody horse throws me off.'

'Yes, sir,' said Bill, stifling a laugh. He looked over at Ernest and nodded furiously. Ernest gave a thumbs-up. 'Right, General, I'll count to five. Then your man must let go of the horse and jump out of the shot. Are you ready?'

'Yes, yes! Just get on with the bloody thing.'

Bill began to count. 'One, two …'

The men joined in and the volume rose with each number. The horse began to panic. White foam ran down its neck where the reins had rubbed, and its front legs stomped. The groom continued to wrestle with the mare to stop it from rearing, but it was a losing battle.

'FOUR, FIVE,' chanted the crowd, drowning Bill's voice.

The groom released the reins and leapt aside. The horse, momentarily stunned by its freedom, stood stock still, its nostrils flared. For the briefest of moments, there was silence as the crowd held a single anticipatory breath.

Ernest pressed the shutter. There was a loud click followed by a flash.

The horse flexed its huge muscles, reared upwards and sprang forward.

The surprised general lurched in the opposite direction on to the horse's back, his feet still in the stirrups but now level with its shoulders. He pulled himself upright with the reins, then, in an act of desperation, wrapped his arms tightly around the horse's neck.

The horse bolted wildly, circling inside the corral of men, who cheered, waved and fought for a better view of the general's misfortune. A cloud of white dust rose in the horse's wake, and some of the soldiers began to cough and choke.

Ernest darted to the side of the ring while Bill and the groom tried to intercept the horse.

On the third lap the horse bucked. The general slid over to one side of the saddle, held on for a few more paces, then slithered unceremoniously into the dirt.

With one voice the crowd gasped, a single intake of breath that stretched and stretched. Then there was silence save the horse's hooves slowing to a halt.

The general heaved himself to his knees and then leant on all fours. Covered in white dust and with the knees of his dress uniform badly ripped, he stood, teetered a step and straightened. Several men ran over to him and brushed away the dust but he shoved them aside.

'Get off me. Get off me,' he said to his men. 'I knew this was a ridiculous idea. This is your fault. You there, holding the horse.'

Bill looked around and pointed at himself.

'Yes, *you*. Report for latrine duty for the next month. Move. NOW.'

'But sir ... it was an amazing photograph. Ernie, tell him, mate.'

'Er, yes, sir,' said Ernest. 'It was, um, quite majestic.' Ernest stared at Bill and then, his mind made up, he continued. 'I'm sure I took the picture just as the horse reared up. You looked like ... well, like Wellington on Copenhagen.'

The general turned to Ernest and slapped his tunic energetically. Dust formed a white cloud in the air.

'Mmm, did I? Yes ... yes, I can see that.'

'And, sir, I have six plates left. Perhaps I could take some more pictures of you standing with your rifle.'

'I see. Yes, yes, very well. It seems a shame to waste them, but be quick about it.'

Bill walked away slowly, hoping to mingle with the crowd.

'Not you. No you don't. I haven't forgotten your part in all this. I could have been killed. Killed, I tell you. Report for latrine duty at twenty-one hundred hours sharp.'

'But, sir ...' The general's face reddened. 'Yes, sir,' Bill said quietly, and then, visibly brightening, 'Right, General, you stand over here with your gun and get into position as if you're about to bayonet the Hun.' Ernest could only smile and shake his head. 'All the dust and rips in your uniform will make it more realistic.'

It was as if the spark that had been quietly travelling down a long fuse finally reached the gunpowder.

'DISMISSED, PRIVATE,' the general bellowed. His voice broke and globules of spit sprayed on to the dusty square. 'I ... AM ... QUITE ... CAPABLE ... OF ... DECIDING ... ON ... MY ... OWN ... POSES. Sergeant ... SERGEANT, make sure this man reports for latrines at twenty-one hundred. DISMISSED.'

Bill turned and quickly disappeared into the crowd.

Though he hated seeing his friend get into trouble, Ernest couldn't help but smile as he prepared his camera.

The general began by practising fighting positions with a fixed bayonet. His men gathered closer around him, offering increasingly outlandish advice, enjoying a rare day of frivolity at the expense of their leader.

'Look more menacing.'

'That's it – stab the Hun.'

'Jump.'

'Growl.'

'Stick your tongue out.'

Howls of laughter followed each suggestion, but the

general seemed oblivious and continued to strike different poses. Ernest took five more photographs before the general grew tired and impatient.

'Right, that's it. I have work to do.' He handed his rifle to a soldier, straightened his back and slapped the dust from his tunic once more. 'Dismiss the men, Sergeant.' He strode over to Ernest, and with his hands clasped behind him, peered down at the diminutive photographer. 'When will the photographs be ready? We must get them sent home without delay.'

Ernest stepped backwards, surprised by the general's proximity.

'Er, I'll need to send them by dispatch rider tomorrow. I don't have any developing equipment here. It'll probably take two or three weeks.'

'TWO OR THREE WEEKS?' thundered the general.

Ernest closed his eyes tightly and moved his head to one side.

'That's an inordinate amount of time, quite ridiculous in this day and age.' He sighed, then slouched forwards. 'Very well, then. Tell me immediately they're ready. Immediately, I say.' And with that he turned on his heels and left the town square. An entourage of soldiers followed in his wake, one or two still trying to brush the dust from the back of his uniform.

Ernest collected his photographic plates and placed them carefully in the canvas bag. The town square was emptying, the soldiers departing for their billets and barracks, but laughter still echoed from the buildings. The sun was now low in the sky and there was a cool breeze, like late afternoon at the seaside, a holiday not ready to end. Something made him look up and although the brightness momentarily dazzled him, the silhouette was unmistakable.

Mira.

She was twenty yards away, her dark hair shimmering with golden flecks. He watched enchanted as she smiled; just the tiniest of movements that lit her face. It took his breath away.

She walked towards him and then, with childlike excitement, she dipped to the ground and picked something up. She straightened, skipped the rest of the way and took Ernest's hands in her own.

'Look, Ernest, look what I've found.' She placed a brown franc on to his palm and closed his fingers around it.

'They say if you find a franc you will have good luck; you have it, Ernest.'

Ernest looked at the coin as if it were the most precious pearl in the ocean. He held it for a moment, trying to feel the essence of Mira's touch, then put it into his pocket.

'Thanks, Mira,' he said, though the words seemed inadequate. 'Quickly. I have one plate left – let me take a photograph of you.'

He took Mira's hand and led her away from the long shadows stretching across the square. He slotted the last plate into the camera and adjusted the viewfinder until he had the beautiful young woman framed. She was laughing.

Ernest clicked the shutter.

He had no idea he would cherish that photograph for the rest of his life.

Bill wandered over. Dust coating his boots as he kicked at some loose stones.

'Bloody hell, latrine duty. Can you bloody believe it?'

Mira and Ernest looked at each other. Mira raised a hand to cover her mouth but couldn't stifle her giggle; it escaped like a tiny bird fluttering into the air. Ernest pressed his lips together but his laughter squeezed through them in a breathy buzz.

'It's not bloody funny,' said Bill crossly.

The three walked back to the farmhouse in a jolly mood though Bill was still annoyed about his punishment.

* * *

The photo shoot with the general had been troubling Ernest for several days but as soon as he'd handed his finished photographic plates to the corporal for dispatch, a weight had lifted from him. Now, the countryside seemed even more beautiful.

They followed the path beside the river, stopping to watch the swallows skimming the water and catching tiny black flies. Bill had refused to carry any of Ernest's equipment as retribution for his laughter and to compensate for the latrine duty, and Ernest breathed heavily as he endeavoured to keep up. Despite this, he was happy; he was in love and for the first time in his life, he felt a connection to the world around him. He marvelled at the trees waving in the breeze and the sunlight reflecting off the river.

'What will you do after the war?' Mira asked him.

'I've told you,' interrupted Bill. 'It's all planned. I'm

going to open a restaurant in London. All the rich and famous people will eat there and Ernie here will take pictures of them. As I always say—'

'Everything happens for a reason,' said Mira and Ernest in unison.

Bill laughed. 'Yes, as I was saying, everything happens for a reason. I've met Ernie here for the publicity and to hobnob with the rich and famous. And now I've met you, Mira.'

'Me?' Mira replied, intrigued. 'What shall I do? Will I entice the gentleman to eat there with my wit and beauty?'

'Er, no,' said Bill, laughing. 'You'll be doing the washing-up.'

Mira squealed and swung her arm towards Bill. He ducked, then dodged her sweeping kick. He ran ahead, all the while looking back, making faces and daring her to chase him. Mira didn't hesitate and was soon in hot pursuit, her laughter blending with the bird song. Bill weaved between the trees, allowing Mira to get close enough to catch him. Then he'd swerve, once more increasing the distance between them.

Ernest struggled with his equipment, and half-walked, half-jogged to keep up.

'Slow down – wait a minute,' he shouted, but Bill and Mira were far ahead and disappeared out of sight as they rounded a corner.

Ernest trudged on, hot and annoyed that his friends had left him behind. By the time he'd reached the farmhouse he was exhausted. Sweat trickled down his back, forming dark, wet patches on his uniform.

The farmhouse looked as picturesque as ever. Blue delphiniums and dark-pink foxgloves battled for prominence with the lavender and white roses. Above the chaos of colour, golden sunflowers swayed with a divine grace, as if looking down on their less important subjects.

Mira and Bill were not waiting for him at the old wooden table. Puzzled, Ernest lowered the canvas bag and camera on to the grass. He wandered to the side of the house and turned the corner.

The view assaulted him.

All the breath left his body and he staggered forward in disbelief.

Mira was in Bill's muscular embrace. His hands pressed her spine, drawing her closer to him. Her face nestled in his neck and she held her arms above her head, elbows bent, hands clasped and falling behind her in surrender.

Held in an evil spell that he doubted would ever be broken, Ernest could not move. In those moments, he told himself he had no claim to Mira that she could do whatever she wished. He wanted to laugh, to be happy for his friends. Anything other than the aching jealousy that raged through his veins. But he couldn't stop himself, and to his shame the words escaped from his lips, feeble with sarcasm.

'Well, it didn't take you two long, did it?' He gulped in several large breaths of air, trying to forestall the tears he knew to be close.

Bill released Mira, startled by Ernest's interruption. 'Ernie … Ernest,' he said as Ernest stumbled backwards.

Mira turned. Ernest looked into her dark eyes and his heart broke.

Tears pooled and streaked her cheeks. Strands of black hair fell wet across her face. In her hand was a single sheet of crumpled white paper. She stood silent. Her mouth, which usually moved so effortlessly into a smile, was thin and stretched. Then it opened and the tiniest note of despair escaped before she ran into the farmhouse.

'You bloody idiot,' hissed Bill. 'She's just found out her dad's been killed.'

Ernest took another step backwards. He shook his head and raised his hands, trying to push away the news.

'No, no. Oh God ... what have I done? I didn't know. I'm so sorry.' Ernest turned towards the farmhouse and Mira's wretched figure.

'Leave her be, Ernie,' said Bill quietly.

'But, Bill, I didn't know. What have I done? Please, Bill ... please.'

'Come here, you daft apeth.'

Bill smiled and Ernest fell into his arms, his shoulders shaking as he surrendered to the grief that overwhelmed him.

* * *

That evening, the candlelight once more flickered on the dull metal pans and cast dancing shadows on the kitchen walls. Over the last couple of weeks, Ernest had looked forward to this part of the day more than any other; it had become a magical hour. Now there was just an air of gloom and the faint sound of muffled sobbing pervading every dusty corner of the farmhouse. Unlike the wailing mourners he'd heard as a boy at his father's funeral, the weeping was soft and gentle but the quietness seemed to heighten the sense of heartbreak rather than lessen it.

Mira's mother sat at the old oak table, whimpering into a tiny embroidered handkerchief. Ernest wondered about that table and the many scars it bore; what sadness and celebration it had seen during its history. Could it distinguish between tears of joy and those of sorrow as they fell on to its pitted surface?

Mira perched on a window ledge, her cheeks etched with the salty lines of her drying tears, her eyes puffy and sore. Her knees were pulled up to her chest, a barrier against the world, and she gazed out of the window at the night sky.

Bill and Ernest sat at the dining table, sipping steaming tea from large white mugs. Through the gloom they watched her, shoulders hunched and twitching with each sob, a tiny animal lost in a bad dream.

'I'm going to have to go, Ernie,' said Bill. 'Latrine duty.'

'Can't you stay, Bill, just this once?' Ernest whispered.

Bill shook his head. 'You know the way it is, Ernie. If I miss this one I'll be scooted up to the front and be in even more trouble. You just make sure Mira's all right. Just ... just look after her, mate.'

They both looked towards her again.

'Stars always look brighter from the kitchen sink,' said Bill quietly. 'But all our dreams must seem pretty hopeless to her at the moment.'

'I can't talk to her,' said Ernest sadly. 'I'm going to bed.'

'Come on, mate. Think of Mira and what's she's going through.'

Ernest shook his head. 'I know. I'm being selfish. I ... I just can't. I don't know what to say.'

'Okay, mate. I got to go. See you in the morning.'

Bill stood up and walked to the front door. Ernest followed, his head down, not daring to look at Mira or her mother. Bill playfully punched him on the shoulder and opened the door. It creaked loudly.

'Night all,' said Bill, and he stepped outside.

Ernest turned to face Mira and her mother.

'Goodnight,' he said. His voice was little more than a whisper but the silence that greeted it was deafening.

As he slowly mounted the stairs he realised again just how quickly things could change.

* * *

Ernest lay in his bed, looking up at the ceiling. He pulled the large quilt over his chin and sunk his head into the soft white pillows. Moonlight shimmered through the curtains on the small window, the slats casting square shadows across the room. He tried to sleep but uninvited thoughts pecked and pulled, swamping his head. After an hour of fitful turning, he opened the curtains and allowed the moonlight to flood over the bed.

The shadows entranced him and after a while, heavy eyed, he drifted towards sleep, only to find himself awake moments later, his head jerking upwards and his eyes wide as he remembered the day's events.

He heard movement on the stairs and propped himself up with the pillows. The bedroom door creaked open slowly, then closed again. A few seconds later it inched open once more, this time wider, the person on the other side tentative and unsure. He watched, astounded, as Mira tiptoed into the moonlight. She closed the door behind her and mouthed *Shhh* before making her way silently to his bed. She took Ernest's fingers in hers and brought them to her lips so that his palm covered her mouth. Then she gently buried her face in his hand and kissed his skin. She retreated a step, letting his fingers fall to the bed, and Ernest saw she was wearing a long white nightshirt buttoned at the front. Slowly, she undid the buttons, not taking her eyes from his, and slipped the shirt over each shoulder. It fell to the ground, revealing her nakedness beneath.

For several moments Ernest almost forgot to breathe. A sharp intake of air turned into an embarrassing gasp. His heart galloped but, tempted as he was, he had neither the courage nor the audacity to take his eyes from Mira's. She tilted her head slightly and Ernest watched her mouth form into a tiny smile.

He glanced at her slender neck and then, with more confidence, followed the line downwards, over her flawless olive skin, to the swell of her breasts that rose and fell in perfect time with each long, deep breath. He felt his excitement building and looked up at Mira's face.

She nodded.

His gaze washed over her body – to her smooth taut stomach, then her legs and thighs, so athletic and lithe. And as his eyes fell at last upon the dark triangle between her legs, the breath left his lungs in a shuddering gasp.

Mira pulled back the quilt, climbed on to the bed and in a single graceful movement straddled Ernest. She held his stare and undid the buttons of his pyjama jacket, brushing it open with her soft hands. She caressed his thin white chest with her fingertips, her touch like a butterfly's kiss.

The feeling was so intense it was almost unbearable. Ernest closed his eyes and willed himself not to call out and pull her fingers away. He trembled with each touch but longed for the next.

Mira leaned forward and placed the tiniest of kisses on first his forehead, then each eyelid, his cheeks and ears. She moved lower to his neck, her hair over his eyes. A breathless murmur escaped Ernest's lips, which Mira quickly smothered, her tongue darting between his lips. She sat back and looked down at him, smiling.

'Touch me,' she whispered. 'Put your hands on me.'

She took Ernest's hands, guided them to her breasts and held them there. Amazed by their softness and how they moved under his fingers, he watched transfixed as she tilted her head backwards and arched her body. Releasing his hands, she reached forward and cradled his head to her chest. She gasped as his warm breath and kisses touched her skin.

She began to move on him, and he grew under her and then inside her.

They held each other tightly, lost in the sensation. Then, clutching his head hard to her breasts, she lifted her hips. The movement was almost imperceptible but it made Ernest look up. Her face was highlighted by moonlight and framed by her luxuriant dark hair, which fell in waves over her shoulders.

Eyes closed, she moved faster and with purpose.

Ernest felt her breath hot on his neck. He lost himself within it and began to move with her, encouraged by the tiny gasps that interrupted her breathing.

Then a sensation spread from his stomach to his thighs and his groin, and he turned inside out as heaven held him, crushed him, drowned him. Surely he would die; surely no one could survive such a feeling. He tried to hold Mira still but she was unstoppable until her breath became ragged in his ear and she, too, gasped and collapsed on to him, her weight forcing him deep into the bed, cocooned and safe in the world.

He pulled her to him, encircling her legs with his, holding on to the moment for as long as he could.

I love you. He sought the words but his voice escaped him, and he buried his face in her hair, ashamed of his cowardice.

They lay entwined, breathing easily now. Ernest stroked her back and watched the shimmering moonlight reflect in the beads of perspiration on their bodies.

He'd never let her go. The moment would last his lifetime.

* * *

When Ernest awoke Mira had gone.

Bill was asleep and snoring in the other bed.

With dismay, Ernest wondered if it had all been a

dream; there was no sign of Mira. Thoughts clamoured in his head.

Why would she come to him? He was an idiot for thinking she would.

Did she feel sorry for him? Did she like him?

Should he say something? But what if nothing had actually happened?

Maybe her father's death had made her crazy. Maybe, maybe, maybe … it was all too much. Whatever the reason, there was no proof that the greatest moment of his life had even taken place.

Ernest sighed and saw with surprise that Bill was standing over his bed.

'What on earth's the matter with you, Ernie, mate? Staring into space like a lunatic. I tell you, you'd have reason to be staring into space if you'd done bloody latrine duty all night, you lucky sod.' Bill pulled the covers away. 'Come on, we need to get up and back into town. Do you want to wash first?'

Ernest stood, yawned and made his way past Bill to the sink.

'Hey, Ernie, you got to stop that bloody cat sleeping on your bed.' Bill plucked a long dark hair from Ernest's pyjamas and held it up to him.

Ernest hurried through the door and turned the corner, out of Bill's sight.

'I know,' he called as the smile stretched wide across his face.

* * *

Bill and Ernest sat outside on the wooden bench, trying to slow the time before they had to report back for duty. Mira brought them strong coffee and crispy white bread, but she hardly spoke. Her eyes were red and puffy and Ernest wondered again if he'd been dreaming.

They ate and drank, lost in their thoughts. The air seemed pure and clean in the early-morning sun. The flowers were all in bloom – blues, reds, yellows and pinks against a canopy of green. Still, despite their beauty, there was an air of melancholy about the farmhouse that no amount of colour could dispel.

Mira slowly clipped the sunflowers, putting the largest ones into a wicker basket. She paused and stared far, far way.

Ernest felt a terrible guilt at his own happiness when Mira was so sad. She seemed so small and fragile, so lost. He wanted to hold her, to keep her safe, but he was buzzing with energy. He was alive, overwhelmed by the desire to sing and dance and tell the flowers of his good fortune. Instead he spoke quietly.

'Why do you cut them? They look so beautiful here in the garden.'

'I want to see them in the house when they are at their most radiant. Soon they will wither and winter will be here. I want to be close to them while they are perfect.'

Ernest fiddled with his small Kodak camera, framing a shot.

'Stand there, Mira. In front of the flowers. Let me take your picture.'

'Non ... No, I don't feel like it.'

'Just one, please. The flowers are so beautiful.'

Mira sighed, put her clippers into her apron pocket, hooked the wicker basket over her shoulder and stood where he'd asked. Ernest got to his feet and positioned himself in front of her. He held the camera up to his chest and peered through the viewfinder, closing one eye.

'Okay. Ready.'

Mira smiled and Ernest clicked the shutter.

'I must put these flowers in water,' she said, her eyes filling, and she pushed open the creaking front door and went into the house.

Mira's departure relieved the tension a little and the men began to relax and enjoy the sunshine. Ernest drifted into a dream as he played with his camera.

'Hey, Ernie, what *is* the matter with you?' Bill prodded Ernest, waking him from his reverie. 'I've never used one of those before,' he said, pointing at the camera. 'Can I take a picture of you?'

'Yes, of course, if you want.' Ernest handed his camera to Bill and lifted the strap over his head. 'Keep the strap round your neck, then you can't drop it. They cost a fortune, you know.' The camera hung by Bill's waist. 'Good. Right, now lift it up, rest it on your chest and look down into that glass viewfinder. You should be able to see me. Hold it steady then slowly push the button on this cord.' Ernest pointed to a brown cable about six inches long with a silver plunger on the end of it.

'I can't see you, mate.' Bill waved the camera from side to side, then up and down.

Ernest laughed. 'No, slowly. Up a little.'

'You must be moving yourself. Keep still, you bugger.'

'It says in the instruction manual that a child can use it. What *are* you doing?' Ernest moved forward to help.

'No … wait, there you are. I have you. Hold still. Here goes.'

Bill squeezed the shutter.

There was a click.

Then the farmhouse exploded.

* * *

For a split second, Bill looked at the camera, unable to comprehend what had happened. Another explosion sent flames and debris spiralling into the air. The blast threw them to the ground. Large fragments of bricks and mortar crashed around, one smashing into Ernest's knee. Bill rose unsteadily to his feet, still stunned.

'Mira!' Ernest cried. 'MIRA!' he shouted again, his voice an animal wail.

'Stay there – I'll get her.'

Bill staggered to the front door. Flames leapt out of the kitchen window, vivid orange, red and yellow. Thick black smoke belched through what remained of the roof, its timber beams splintered and scattered haphazardly in the garden. Bill pushed at the front door but it wouldn't budge. He took a step back and kicked it hard, three times, until finally it gave way.

A curtain of flames engulfed him. He felt himself lifted, the inferno cradling him for a moment before flinging him, flame-soaked, to the ground. Once more he staggered to his feet, his face black, smoke curling into the air from his ripped and smouldering uniform.

He reached the door, kicked away the few remaining fragments of wood blocking his path and turned to Ernest with a small smile of reassurance that failed to disguise the wince from his charred lips. With a final deep breath and his arm covering his mouth, he crashed through the doorway and disappeared into the farmhouse.

Ernest struggled to his feet, dazed by the explosion. The pain in his knee was excruciating. He hobbled to the door, shaking his head to clear it. All around him the ground shook as rockets soared through the air. The noise was beyond deafening; he couldn't think straight and moved with leaden limbs. The whistle of mortars screamed around him, a cacophony of cries in a sky of fire …

* * *

He had no recollection of losing consciousness but he woke, bewildered, to find himself sprawled face down in the dirt and covered in wood and concrete. He had no idea how much time had elapsed. And despite his efforts, the farmhouse seemed further away. Pain, fear, sadness and horror contorted his face and once more he began to stagger towards the burning building.

The farmhouse exploded again as several more mortars found their target, sending the walls, roof and windows skyward in a frenzy of flame. Ernest was lifted from the ground and flung twisting into a tree. He fell through the boughs until his boots became wedged between two branches.

There he hung with half-closed eyes under a veil of green against a smoke-black sky. And before all awareness left him, he saw the last two sunflowers waving defiantly until the flames found their golden heads.

* * *

Ernest came to, still upside down in the tree. Using the last of his strength he pulled himself upright, twisted the branches away from his boots and fell heavily on to his back. The impact took the wind from his lungs. He lay on the grass, at peace for a moment, as the blood returned to his tingling limbs.

Gingerly, he sat up and looked across at the smouldering farmhouse. He limped to the doorway. Black smoke still curled from the building and he tentatively made his way inside.

The rooms were unrecognisable. The walls were gone. The beautiful old oak beams that had once lined the kitchen, lay blackened and shattered next to buckled metal pots that had seemed so indestructible. The stairwell had collapsed and through the smoke it took Ernest several breaths to comprehend what he was looking at.

He let loose a miserable, childlike wail. 'No, no, no, no … NO!'

Protruding from the bricks were two uniformed legs, blackened by the flames. Ernest fell to the floor whispering a desperate prayer for the impossible. He clawed at the rubble, nails breaking on the bricks, refusing to accept the futility of his actions.

There was no hope.

Each slab removed brought the smell of death, darker and deeper, and finally he stopped when he could lift no more and his fingers were raw. He knelt and cried, his tears dissolving into the red stains on the floor.

More of the stairwell collapsed in a plume of white dust. He waved his hand in front of his face to clear the choking fog. As it settled he stared, uncomprehending, at an oval shape lying close to Bill. He leaned forward and moved his head a few inches nearer, squinting, trying to remember. Then with a cry of recognition he scrambled backwards up the mound of rubble, kicking against the bricks.

Mira's wicker basket. It was black now, the sunflowers carbonised, their leaves floating dark fragments. Through the wreckage a small charred hand still held the handle.

He vomited.

Then, in the dust and debris and puke, he curled into a ball and sobbed and retched again and again until the last of the bile dribbled down his chin and the only thing left to spew was the shit from his bowels.

He could endure no more, and sleep took him.

* * *

The bombardment resumed. The shaking ground and whistling mortars returned Ernest, who had been dreaming of home, to his nightmare.

He scrambled over the rubble and out of the house, hobbling through the fields, tripping and falling until he finally found the British lines.

* * *

In the ensuing weeks Ernest refused all offers of help. He became a recluse living at one end of a disused trench, oblivious to the mud that encrusted his uniform and matted his hair.

An unquenchable hatred raged within him, an abhorrence of all living things.

He volunteered for every mission and the opportunity to wreak revenge on the enemy. He would be the first over the top, leading the charge across no man's land and the last to return, reluctant, and disappointed that a bullet hadn't found its mark.

He had no fear of death; he'd nothing more to lose. And, as is the strange way of the world, he remained unscathed, while those who cherished life or had families praying for them perished.

His platoon kept their distance and called him Mad Ernie, but secretly he became their talisman and the men watched his every move, talking in admiring whispers about this strange, silent maverick.

One cold February night, Ernest volunteered for a raid behind enemy lines. Headquarters had received intelligence of an imminent German push and the mission was to establish if there was a build-up of troops or weapons.

He was part of a small group of men that slipped across no man's land, under the cover of clouds that cloaked the moonlight. They followed a route used for previous incursions and reached an abandoned trench close to enemy lines, where they rested and planned their next move.

Ernest remained silent throughout, offering no comfort to his inexperienced companions. He no longer thought about home, his mother or his friends. Numb and broken he wished only that his weary legs would give up the fight so he could rest in the mud for a final time.

The sergeant was pointing to various targets on the map but Ernest could not hide his distain. This was his fourth mission and each had followed an identical route. So he was unsurprised and partly relieved when on this freezing night, as the men huddled together, the enemy swarmed into the trench in a carefully choreographed ambush.

In a breath they surrounded the squad, and when the maelstrom had subsided men on both sides lay dead or dying.

Ernest opened his eyes – pinned beneath a heavy torso he was barely able to move. He could feel blood, dripping warm through his tunic. In the narrow confines of the trench, the German numbers had been of little consequence; there was only room for one or two to challenge at a time and both forces had found equal success. Ernest pushed his way through the tangle of legs and on one knee, like a frenzied butcher he surveyed the scene.

The trench was chaos, with bodies piled one atop another. Some still gasped for air as blood filled their lungs; others lay, limbs akimbo, the life already snuffed out of them.

Ernest spotted a movement towards the end of the trench. In the shadows a young German soldier cowered against the muddy wall. Ernest raised his bayonet just as the young man turned and held his gaze.

Something shimmered on the German's chest and Ernest saw a small tin whistle in his top pocket, glinting in the dark. The young man raised his shaking hands, palms out, fingers slightly bent, ready for death. But Ernest's eyes would not be drawn from the whistle. He remembered his camera and his love of photography and wondered what joy that whistle had brought the young German. He lowered the bayonet and closed his eyes, wishing for the war to end, to be taken away from this hell, to be the boy he'd once been and would never be again. A single tear traced a line down his soot-covered cheek and dropped to a bloody puddle. He watched the ripple begin its journey.

The skies filled once more with colour and noise.

Aware of the ambush, the British artillery had targeted their position. Mortars crashed around them, sending mud and bodies spiralling into the air like macabre gymnasts. Ernest grabbed the German soldier and flung him to the end of the trench where a small parapet offered protection. Seconds later a rocket exploded where he'd been lying, lifting Ernest heavenwards. He crashed to the earth, landing awkwardly, his legs buckling under his weight.

Ernest sank and cried into the mud. Perhaps now was the time to say *enough*, to lie still and embrace death. His limbs were limp, his soul empty.

Then, when he had nothing left, he felt the gentlest of touches under his arms, encouraging him to his feet. Ernest felt sure it was the devil, lifting him from the battlefield and taking him home, but as he turned his head he saw the young German cradling him. In that field, they held each other as lovers might have done many years before, when it was still beautiful, and together they staggered towards the British lines.

The fire crackle blast of machine guns fractured the air. Flares floated to the ground, their eerie light highlighting the zip and zing of bullets as they hit the earth inches from Ernest and his rescuer.

'Don't shoot. British,' Ernest rasped. Then louder. 'DON'T SHOOT ... DON'T SHOOT ... I'M BRITISH.'

The machine guns halted. The German, caught like a rabbit in a headlight, lowered Ernest to his knees and then gently on to his side. He took five paces backwards, staring straight at the British guns, arms half-raised, then turned and scurried back to his own lines.

* * *

Ernest woke in a rickety hospital bed. His legs were in plaster and suspended from a pulley system comprising battered brown weights attached to yellowing, well-used cords. It was a makeshift field hospital, no more than a large tent with two rows of five beds. The thin green canvas failed to keep out the icy wind, and the dull thump of artillery fire could be heard some miles away.

Ernest looked around the room; a wounded soldier occupied each bed. Some had limbs missing or dark, festering burns open to the air. Bandages covered others and Ernest dared not think what lay hidden beneath those tight white shrouds. The low, wretched groans of hopelessness were unceasing.

On a small table near his bed a vase of dried sunflowers

tried to cheer the forlorn tent. The petals were dry yellow husks, all life sucked from them, and he remembered painfully the vibrant green and gold of Mira's garden, which was now gone.

As the weeks passed, Ernest noticed that if he lay low in his bed, he could look between the sunflowers so that their stems and leaves hid the rest of the tent and he could imagine he was somewhere else. He would while away the long hateful hours until a young nurse would appear, as if by magic, to tend him.

He knew her only as Nurse Fisher. She fluttered efficiently about the ward like a little bird and spoke softly with a faint London accent. Her hair was always tied tightly behind her nurse's bonnet but Ernest imagined it was long and dark. Above all else, she was kind and he never failed to be charmed by her patience and care.

He spoke to Nurse Fisher every day. She told him about the night of his injury and how a German soldier had carried him halfway across no man's land to safety. They talked about England, their old lives and their plans for the future. And Ernest told her about Bill and Mira. Little snippets at first. Then, like the mortars, the words exploded from him.

He told her about Bill's restaurant and his unwavering belief that everything happened for a reason; about Mira and her poetry; about Mira's father and the lucky franc, which he proudly showed her. As he spoke he remembered his friends as alive and vital, and in time, with her help, he found a space in which to laugh again.

His legs were improving and he was preparing for a

few weeks leave when a battered brown parcel arrived, its paper torn and dirty. White padding poked through the rips and a patchwork of inky scrawls covered the front of the parcel – old addresses had been crossed through and new locations added. The latest had finally found him in his hospital bed.

Curious, Ernest carefully removed the wrapping paper and found, to his surprise, photographic prints. He placed them on his lap and turned the first one over. The general stared back, looking the complete antithesis of the heroic London statues he'd so wanted to emulate. He sat astride the big nervous horse. The next photographs were of the general in various poses, his bayonet poised and his uniform ripped and dusty. Ernest could almost hear the men goading him into more preposterous positions. The last picture lay on his bed. He turned it over slowly and reverently.

Mira.

She was beautiful. She stood in the town square in her white shirt; her dark hair tied back, the sunlight igniting her smile so that it shone from the print.

His hands shook and he dropped the picture. A small, silent intake of breath turned into a sob, then an uncontrollable wail. His shoulders shook through the torrent of tears like a child's and he covered his face with his hands to hide his embarrassment.

He wept for Mira and Bill and all those beautiful young men who had once been small boys, who'd played games and felt safe within their mothers' arms.

All broken now.

The pity and injustice of the world splintered him to his core. His sorrow knew no bounds and the flow of tears would not be stemmed until Nurse Fisher held his face tightly in her hands and refused to let it go. She looked into his eyes and implored him to come back to the world, and when Ernest shut them tightly, his skin creasing with the effort, she kissed him hard on the lips.

His eyes sprung open in surprise. When he'd regained his breath and found the beginning of a smile, he asked her name.

'Violet,' she said quietly, caressing his face. 'I'm Violet.'

CHAPTER TWENTY-ONE

Warm Sunflowers

1972

The sitting room had become gloomy as the late-afternoon sun fell beneath the tree line. The two men sat in silence. Ernest rubbed his forehead while Raymond struggled to find the words to comfort his friend.

'So there you have it,' said Ernest after a while. 'Not much honour or bravery from me, I'm afraid.'

'Ernest, I—'

'Shh,' interrupted Ernest, holding up a defensive palm. 'There's nothing more to say. I could have helped Bill and Mira. I didn't move.'

'You'd been stunned by the bombs – you couldn't move.'

'It didn't stop Bill, did it?'

'But ... Ernest, I'm so sorry.'

'It was a long time ago, but I can't forget. I've tried to live every day for the moment. Tried to be kind and follow a dream or two. Maybe that's what Bill's death was meant to teach me, but in my heart I know it's all rubbish.' He shook his head slowly, his eyes closed. 'He was a fine young man with a whole wonderful life ahead of him and he died for nothing. And I didn't try to save him. And Mira—' Ernest's voice broke.

'You couldn't do anything. Don't say that – you didn't have a choice.'

'Everyone has a choice, Raymond.'

There was an uncomfortable silence. Raymond sat frustrated, the right words evading him. Ernest stared at the wall, gazing into his old photograph.

'I don't know, I think you're being too hard on yourself. And something good did come out of it – you met Violet and spent – how long was it? Fifty years?' Ernest nodded. 'Fifty years together. That's got to be good, hasn't it?'

Raymond got up from his armchair and walked over to Ernest.

'I've got to go now.'

Ernest continued to sit rigidly in his chair, lost in thought, his hands gripping the arms. Raymond gently touched Ernest's white fingers and let himself out.

'See you soon. Bye, Ernest.'

* * *

That evening, Raymond watched the night sky through his bedroom window. His view of the world had changed. The same stars shone on the same earth but the reality of life hurt him. He could see the sadness that many endured so stoically and the impossible decisions, made in a moment, which could affect them for the rest of their lives. He felt small; a tiny part of the universe; his life brief and hopelessly insignificant.

What was the point? What was the fucking point?

He slumped on to his bed and curled into a ball, hedgehog safe. He glanced downwards and there on the floor, golden in the dreary electric night-light, he saw his sunflower book. Ernest's words, spoken with such sadness came back to him, a flash of colour in a barren and bleak world.

'Be kind and follow a dream or two.'

In that moment his soul, if he had one, wrapped itself around those words and held them as if they were the most fragile flowers in winter, keeping them warm and safe and ready for the rest of his life. He snuggled under the blankets and put his hands together.

'Gentle Jesus, meek and mild, look upon a little child. Pity my simplicity. Suffer me to come to thee. God bless Mum and Dad, nannies, granddads, aunties, uncles, cousins John and Clive, and all kind friends, and make Ray a good boy, for Jesus' sake. And, Lord, please look after Ernest and make him happy again. He's been through an awful lot. Amen.'

* * *

The next few days saw the weather change. Black clouds hung in the sky and rain splashed the pavements. Raymond stayed indoors, read his books and attempted to write some poetry. He found a new voice at home and talked to his parents about the news, current affairs and, for the first time, their lives. They enjoyed reliving the past, and Raymond grew to understand that they too had been young, with fears and dreams similar to his own.

Then, on the Friday, the sun peeked shyly through the clouds, an early-morning apology for the days of dreariness. Raymond ambled down the stairs, feeling happy as the sunlight blazed his way to the kitchen. He would have breakfast and then visit Ernest.

He sat at the kitchen table, engrossed in a new book, blindly spooning cornflakes into his mouth, the milk splattering back into the bowl. His dad had long since departed for work and his mum washed the crockery left in the sink from the night before.

'What you reading, Ray?' she said.

'It's just a poetry book; William Wordsworth. Ernest likes one of the poems.'

'Poetry!' his mum laughed. 'Goodness, you have changed. I didn't think you liked that sort of thing.'

'Yeah, I always liked the First World War poets, Mum, remember? I did it for my A level.'

'Yes, that rings a bell,' said his mum. 'I like the new you. Er, not that I didn't like the old you.' She smiled.

'Thanks, Mum … I think.' Raymond grinned and they held each other's gaze for a few moments.

'By the way, did you know your sunflowers are out?'

'*What?*' Raymond leapt from his chair, dropping the poetry book. 'Why didn't you say? My sunflowers are out!' He ran to the hallway and tried to put on his shoes without undoing the laces.

'Raymond, you'll ruin them. Give them here.' His mum took the shoes. He watched as she worked, her head lowered in concentration, her kindness instinctive. He felt himself glow, lit by her love.

He slid on his shoes and without bothering to tie up the laces burst through the front door, barely keeping his balance as he rushed into the garden. The sun bathed him in yellow and he breathed in the smell of freshly mown grass. He was halfway down the path when he saw them and stopped.

Four glorious sunflowers.

They stood majestic, nodding gently in the light breeze, shafts of sunlight reflecting off their golden heads. Raymond approached them solemnly and looked into the blue sky. The huge yellow flowers swayed above him, ragged silhouettes momentarily blocking the brightness from his eyes.

He raised his hands to the sky and stretched his fingers. Quietly at first, then louder, he celebrated with whoops and shouts, oblivious to the neighbour's twitching curtains. He spun on the spot, round and round until he noticed the uninvited surveillance.

'Look at the flowers! Look at the flowers!' And then quietly to himself, he said, 'Ernest.'

He pulled open the garden gate and dashed down the road. To his joy a bus was waiting at the stop, the last person just about climb on to the rear platform. He sprinted and leapt, landing in front of the conductor.

'Morning,' he said happily, and took his seat.

The journey seemed interminable. At every stop

passengers struggled and bumbled, their shopping bags either primed in readiness or full to bursting, so that progress along the narrow aisle was excruciating.

As the bus neared Ernest's road, the conductor followed an elderly couple up the stairs, tutting at their laboured efforts to get to the top deck. Unperturbed by her absence, Raymond reached forward, rang the bell and negotiated his way off the bus, a jubilant smile illuminating his face.

CHAPTER TWENTY-TWO

A Poem

He ran the rest of the way to Ernest's house at such a speed that he misjudged the distance to the front door and clattered into it. He banged on it with his open hands, face pressed against the glass.

'Ernest, Ernie!' he shouted. 'Open the door. My sunflowers are out. Hurry up – you've got to see them.'

Raymond continued to knock loudly on the door, then pressed the bell repeatedly, but no one answered.

There was no sign of life and Raymond took a step backwards, puzzled. He moved to the front window and peered through the net curtains.

'Can I help you?' said a man behind him.

Raymond jumped and turned, his face flushing.

'What's all this noise? Is everything all right?'

Raymond looked around but saw no one. Then he noticed one of Ernest's neighbours, an elderly man in a thick grey cardigan, leaning over the fence.

'Yes, everything's fine,' said Raymond. 'I need to find Ernest. Do you know where he is?'

'Ah, I know you. You're Ernest's young friend, aren't you? He's done nothing but talk about you. It's Raymond, isn't it? Yes?'

Raymond nodded.

'Well, he goes on and on about you. It's Raymond this and Raymond that. Oh, I do hope he's all right.'

'What do you mean?' said Raymond, a hollow feeling growing in the pit of his stomach.

'Oh dear, he had a dreadful fall. He was taken off in an ambulance to the new place. He was unconscious, all strapped to a stretcher. He's in there now. I haven't heard anything else.'

'Oh no ... When ... when was this? Is he all right?'

'Must have been four or five days ago.'

'Oh God, no. I ... I must be going. I'm sorry. Thank you.'

Raymond dashed down the path and ran back to the bus stop. He didn't know what to do and had no idea where the new hospital was. His only thought was to get home – perhaps his mum and dad could help.

The bus ride was uneventful but Raymond was so preoccupied that he almost missed his stop and had to ring the bell at the last moment, much to the annoyance of the conductor.

He walked back to his house feeling helpless and deflated. His mind whirled with every awful possibility. He kicked a stone hard across the road, sending it clattering against the opposite kerb.

'Careful, Mr Bender. That could've been dangerous.'

The cold, menacing voice made Raymond look up with a start.

'Glad we bumped into you, or should I say Mr Bumped into you?'

The skinheads walked towards him, their cruel laughter echoing in his deadened ears. They surrounded him and patted him on the back.

'Still no poofter friend, I see. That's such a shame. But, look, Roy here says he reckons you caught that poofter stuff from your pussy flowers. So, my friend, we've been doing our civic duty to help you.' The skinhead spat on the pavement in front of Raymond's feet and raised his hands in mock surrender. 'No, no ... it's okay, please ... don't thank us.'

They were laughing hard now. Roy raised a long branch and pointed the end at Raymond's face.

Raymond's eyes focused on squashed flecks of gold clinging to the bark. He looked at the thugs in horror, not believing what they seemed to be telling him.

'No,' he said, barely whispering. He closed his eyes, not wanting to see anymore. 'No.' He pushed past them and ran for home as if his life depended on it. He heard the skinheads' calls of *eeeew* behind him, though he no longer had any thought for them. He ran until he was convinced his heart would explode, until there was no air left in his lungs. Then, as he turned the corner he saw them. A host of yellow petals, dancing gently across the street.

He walked slowly to his house, thoughts of Ernest and the wrecked sunflowers drowning him with every step.

The act of putting one foot in front of the other took all his willpower and as he neared his garden wall, his rasping breath smothered the sounds of the outside world.

The sunflowers were all but gone.

One, broken in the middle, folded sharply downwards, the flower hanging by a single sliver of stem. The others stood beheaded, their beautiful golden crowns stark and lifeless on the green lawn. Petals blew about the garden and the leaves lay scattered in the borders.

He opened the front gate. His mother knelt in front of the flowers, clutching bamboo poles and a ball of green string. She supported the remains of the sunflowers as best she could, gently untwisting their mangled stems and binding them precariously to the poles. The gate creaked and she looked up. Sorrow etched her face, pulling her thin lips taut.

'Raymond.' She stood and moved towards him, her hand outstretched.

He shook his head. 'No, Mum, I can't. Ernest is in hospital. He's had a really bad fall and now … I just …'

'Raymond, come here.' Then the words registered. 'Ernest is in hospital?' She reached out to touch his hand. Their eyes met. He could see her concern but couldn't bring himself to move his fingers to hers. He sidestepped her attempted hug and pushed through the front door.

'Sorry, Mum, I just can't. I need to get inside.'

'Okay, Ray,' she said. 'We'll talk about it later.' And then she added quietly, her voice breaking, 'Love you.'

* * *

Raymond spent the rest of the afternoon in his bedroom, cocooned under his blankets, dozing and thinking. Later, he tried to find the hospital's number in the telephone directory but couldn't decide which department he should ask for. In frustration he tossed the heavy book aside. It thumped loudly on the floor.

As dusk gave way to darkness, his bedroom light burned against the night, but the harsh yellow glow only added to the melancholy that hung in the air, feeding on the silence. Raymond felt stuffy and bored. Everything irritated him; even his lightweight nylon sheets felt heavy on his skin. He switched off the light and wondered why God, Jesus, the Holy Ghost and everyone else he knew in heaven had made things so horrible despite his prayers.

What had he done?

He racked his brains for an answer but couldn't think of anything. Above all, he wished he'd gone to see Ernest sooner, despite the rainy weather. He closed his eyes, put his hands together and began to recite the familiar words. He offered extra prayers if Ernest came home in the next couple of days and said how sorry he was for anything he'd done that might have brought about the day's awful events.

He felt a little easier then, but sleep still eluded him. His head spun, weaving the recent months' memories. He lay on one side, then the other, trying to find a cooler, more comfortable position.

An hour later, he switched on the bedside lamp, reached into his cupboard and rummaged around for a small blue writing pad. He began to jot down his thoughts and soon the pages were full of doodles, scribbles and crossings-out.

Raymond became engrossed. He sat upright, leaning against his pillows, the notepad resting on his bended knees. Slowly, sentences emerged, creeping down the page. The minutes dissolved into hours. Shadows flickered around his pencil and on to the paper as he worked on his words.

Finally, his lips moved noiselessly as he read. He smiled and placed the notepad on the bedroom floor, switched off the light and closed his eyes.

Within moments sleep held him safe, transporting him to the place where dreams began ...

> *A seagull floating on the summer's breeze above a rocky promontory, waves washing through a natural arch releasing white seahorses of foam. And far, far below, a family raced across the sand ...*

Silver shafts of moonlight streamed through the curtains and made their silent journey across the floor. They tiptoed on to the notepad and illuminated Raymond's words with their soft glow.

> *Moments make and move the magic of the day.*
> *Some shine and sparkle, others softly fade away.*
> *But most precious of all are those that linger and enhance,*
> *Soaring forever in the hallowed hallways of our hearts.*

The next morning, Raymond woke feeling ready to tackle the world. Despite his troubled sleep, a spontaneous smile erupted across his face. As he kicked off the covers and leapt out of bed he noticed the writing pad lying on the floor. And he remembered.

A joyless weight descended and he slumped on his bed looking hard at the white ceiling.

After a while he mooched downstairs and into the kitchen. His parents sat blowing into their steaming mugs of coffee. They looked at each other with concern and Raymond's dad nodded towards his wife.

'Ray, there you are. Dad phoned the hospital last night,' she said. 'Ernest's all right. He's just had a nasty fall – broke his ankle and banged his head. He was unconscious for a while.' She glanced at her husband again. He returned her gaze with wide eyes and smiled supportively. 'The only thing is, he's been moved to Birmingham. They needed the bed so he's gone to a rest home ... just while he recovers,' she added hastily. 'He couldn't go back to his own house by himself with no one to look after him. Apparently, he's got a brother who lives up there and they thought it would be good for him to be near his family.'

'What?' said Raymond, confused. 'He's okay? But ... but been moved to Birmingham?'

'Yes.'

'But that's miles away. I won't see him for ages. When will he be home?'

'The main thing is, Ernest's all right. And Birmingham isn't that far away. Maybe we can visit,' said his dad.

'But Dad, I ... I ...' The words wouldn't come. Ernest was all right, but Birmingham? What was he doing there?

His relief was buried beneath the thought that he might never see Ernest again.

'Look, I have his address here. Write to him; tell him we'll visit in a couple of weeks.'

'But, Dad, it's miles away. How will I get there?'

'We'll go in the car. I'm owed some leave. We'll make a long weekend of it.' His dad was smiling now. 'It'll be an adventure, like we used to have. Write to him, Ray. Ask if it's okay and I'll book my leave.'

Raymond looked at his parents. They seemed small and somehow older. He felt in his heart their concern and love for him; they were both desperate to make things right, to care for him as they'd always done. If they wrapped him in their warmth, everything would be all right.

He moved closer, feeling their arms around him. And for the first time in a decade he surrendered.

CHAPTER TWENTY-THREE
The Letter (Part One)

Raymond sat in his room. Now more positive, he began to compose a letter to Ernest. At first he struggled to find the words, but gradually they wound their way down his pen and on to the paper.

> *Dear Ernest,*
> *I was so sorry to hear about your fall and that you have been in hospital. It was such a shock when your neighbour gave me the news. I went to your house to tell you that for the first time EVER my sunflowers are out. They look beautiful. It's all down to your help and advice — it's never happened before!*
>
> *Apart from that, nothing else has really changed here. We're all worried about you and I miss our chats. Dad has said we can visit in a couple of weeks; he's owed some time off work. We'll probably come on a Thursday or Friday and stay for the weekend. Is that all*

right? Are we allowed? Please let me
know ASAP.

Remember when we first met outside
the DHSS? It seems like a world away. I
feel like such a different person now. SO
MUCH has changed, all for the better,
and once again it's all down to you. But
I want to have some more adventures.
Please get well and come home soon.

Last night I was thinking about
what we've done since that day at the
dole office and I wrote some words
(or rather Dougal Hyland wrote them,
haha). I'll put them in with this letter.
It's a start, and it's for you, Ernest.
Let me know what you think.

I worry so much about your fall. Was
it my fault for making you chase the
coin down the hill? I know you really
hurt your leg — I shouldn't have gone on
about it. I am so sorry, Ernest.

Finally, when you read my poem you'll
know what I mean. You'll always walk
in the hallways of my heart and I will
forever follow your advice — be kind and
have a dream or two.

Best wishes. See you soon.

Your friend,
Raymond

Raymond folded the letter into quarters and put it in an
envelope. He was about to lick the seal when he remembered his poem and retrieved the notepad from the floor.

He carefully removed the page and slid it between the folds of the letter.

His mum, who always seemed to own exactly what Raymond needed, provided a stamp, then handed him his coat. He pulled it on and walked out into the morning.

Thunderclouds skimmed the sky and the air held the bite of an autumn breeze. Raymond trudged down the garden path and forced himself to look at his sunflowers.

Three broken green stalks stood before him. To the side of the wall a single flower remained, held up by the makeshift splint his mother had assembled. A sliver of green miraculously carried the sap between the two pieces of stem, and against all the odds the sunflower waved tall, proud and golden against the dark sky. Raymond stood in front of it for several minutes, watching the large yellow head nod heavily in the quickening breeze. Though acute sadness engulfed him, thick and dark, shrouding everything in shadow, in the flower he found a pinprick of joy. Bewildered, the smallest of smiles slipped on to his lips.

He posted his letter, then caught the bus into town and wandered around the shops.

Before he'd met Ernest, shopping hadn't interested Raymond. Lately, though, he'd begun to take more care with his appearance and found himself drawn towards the red SALE signs that hung in many of the shop windows. He'd discovered good-quality clothes for the same price as his old baggy bargain-basement gear. His wardrobe had expanded, much to his mother's approval. Today, though, nothing tweaked his interest, and he meandered along the streets, daydreaming.

A steady drizzle saturated his coat, intensifying the cool breeze that blew around the street corners. After an hour, he decided to go home. As he neared his bus stop, an Interflora on the other side of the road caught his eye. On the pavement large silver tubs burst with an assortment of colourful blooms and he crossed over to take a closer look. One of the tubs contained ready-made bouquets of white chrysanthemums, lilies and pink roses. A special-offer sign was pinned above.

On impulse – one that even Raymond himself thought uncharacteristic – he bought a bunch for his mother.

The bus trip home was the usual busy affair but these journeys no longer held any fear. He thought about the days he'd prayed the conductor would stay on his floor so he didn't have to ring the bell, and of all the stops he'd missed because of his anxiety. It all seemed so long ago. The gentle rhythm of the bus now soothed him. How things had changed in just a few months. Content, he sat and people-watched, wedged close to the window by a large, puffing elderly man in too many clothes.

An image of Ernest in the trenches came to him – frightened and covered in mud. It contrasted starkly with the warm cosy bus. At the time, his own fear had felt so real and overwhelming, but now, comparing it to what those young soldiers had endured he felt a duty to face whatever adversity came his way.

Raymond smiled and felt part of this microcosm of humanity; so many hopes and dreams, what ifs and if onlys. He felt safe, optimistic even, and wondered why every wish in the world couldn't come true. He was no longer afraid; it was as though Ernest cradled him, and he was certain his friend would never let him fall whatever sorrow or surprises life offered.

When he arrived home and gave the flowers to his mother, her eyes glistened with tears. She held her nose close to the bouquet to hide her embarrassment, before hurrying into the kitchen to put them in a vase.

The next week dragged slowly by.

Every morning, Raymond waited with his mother for the post. But with each day that failed to bring news of Ernest, their disappointment became harder to bear.

He continued to write, jotting ideas on to his crowded notepad. He enjoyed sitting in the quiet of his room, thinking about the right phrase, and a page in his pad often contained more crossings-out than words. But slowly poems and stories emerged. He smiled as he read them back to himself, mystified as to where they'd come from.

Raymond signed on as usual, relieved that the dole office was quiet. The thugs no longer frightened him and in the absence of his fear their interest in him waned. He'd moved on; he was no longer scared of the world. He knew there would be good and bad in his life and that he needed to embrace both.

He gathered his courage and spoke to one of the clerks about journalism and library work. The clerk, happy that someone had shown interest, gave Raymond a sheaf of leaflets, job vacancies and information on courses. He replaced Raymond's lost giro and directed him to a notice about a DHSS recruitment drive. He said it was a good place to work, had a brilliant social club and thought Raymond would fit in well.

Raymond left delighted, the cosy glow of possibility warming his heart.

On his way home, he visited The Salt Shaker. He sat at the usual small table and looked around. Nothing had changed – the white walls, the tiny tables covered by blue floral cloths, the greasy iron griddle, and blackboard menu with the exotic chilli con carne.

His life was so different yet the world continued around him, unaffected.

He and Keith chatted about Ernest – happy tales. Keith knew more about Ernest's later life, how he'd snapped the rich and famous and had many of his photographs published in the society papers of the day, even *Time* magazine.

Raymond stared quietly at his coffee, regretting not asking Ernest more about his career.

Keith seemed to sense his discomfort.

'It's typical of Ernest not to talk about his success.' He paused and took a deep breath. 'I'm going to close this place.'

'What ... why?' asked Raymond, stunned.

'Oh, the fast-food chains are on their way in and trade is slow. People just don't want to wait for a quality hand-cooked burger these days.' He smiled.

'But you've been here for as long as I can remember. I always wondered what chilli con carne was.' Raymond shook his head.

Keith chuckled. 'Yes. If I had a pound for every time

someone has asked that I'd be a rich man.' He looked at Raymond. 'But it's time to move on.' There was sadness in his voice. 'You know, sometimes your dreams don't work out and sometimes they do. The important thing is to have them. I think Ernest and I have had plenty of dreams and we've even managed to live a few. That's what's important. Hang on a sec.'

Keith stood up and moved behind the counter. He returned with a white polystyrene cup full of steaming chilli con carne.

'Try it. On the house. It might be your last chance.'

Raymond looked at Keith, not quite believing what was happening. He was friends with the owner of a cafe and he was being given, for free, the mysterious food that had intrigued him since he was a small child. Tentatively, he dipped a plastic spoon into the cup and brought the chilli to his lips. It was hot, not just spicy, and Raymond gulped some of the water Keith had brought to the table. He could feel the bite and burn of the chilli as it warmed his stomach.

He gasped. 'Wow. This is … goodness.' He hiccupped between laughing.

'You never know what you might be missing until you try it, Raymond.' Keith touched his nose with a finger and winked.

Keith served his other customers while Raymond finished his meal. The spoon made white lines in the bottom of the cup as he scraped the last few morsels into his mouth.

As he stood to leave, Keith came over and for an

awkward moment held Raymond's shoulders. Then they shook hands, neither wanting the embrace to end.

Raymond left The Salt Shaker with a peculiar mix of emotions – elated that Ernest had pursued a successful career but sad that he'd not found out more about it. The news of the cafe's closure was a shock. He remembered the tiny building from his childhood; he'd wander around the town, hand in hand with his mother, who'd hurry past without a second glance. A forbidden fruit, part of his history, and it was closing for good. Some things changed, and some things stayed the same.

There was no pattern and he felt baffled by it all.

* * *

Each evening, Raymond lay in bed reading and writing. Once he'd switched off the lights, he began his familiar routine.

'Gentle Jesus, meek and mild ...'

He'd said those words so many times they were now instinctive; he felt strange on the rare occasions he forgot to say them. Years ago, wrapped up in bed against the cold at his nan's house in East London, he'd screwed his eyes tightly shut, clenched his tiny hands together and recited the lines with his mother. The prayer had evolved into a chant, an incantation, and he was sure its magic had helped him with exams, doctors, even the bus. It had lengthened over the years as he'd added cousins and friends. He still remembered his nan and granddad in the words even though they'd died several years earlier.

For the past five nights Raymond had added a heartfelt plea to the end of the prayer.

'And, Lord, please make it come tomorrow. Forty prayers if Ernest's letter comes tomorrow. Holy Ghost, everyone, please help. Forty prayers, I promise. And please look after Ernest. God bless. Amen.'

* * *

Raymond woke the next morning feeling drowsy. He'd overslept by more than an hour.

He heard the clatter of cups as his mum tidied in the kitchen. Then the letter box rattled and there was a thump as envelopes hit the mat.

'Raymond,' his mum called up the stairs. 'Ray, I think there's something here from the home.'

'Yes!' Raymond laughed. He leapt out of bed, pulled on his dressing gown and rushed down the stairs two at a time.

'Forty prayers tonight. Thank you, Lord,' he whispered as he ran into the kitchen.

A white envelope with Caulfields Care Home elegantly printed above the address lay on the kitchen table. He stopped and looked at it for a few moments, not quite believing it had arrived, then tore it open.

Inside was a neatly typed letter. Raymond began to read.

'Mum,' he whispered. 'Mum …'

CHAPTER TWENTY-FOUR
The Letter (Part Two)

Dear Mr Mann,
I am sorry to inform you that your
friend Ernest Gardiner passed away this
afternoon. There were complications
following his recent fall.

While he was with us he talked about
you every day. Your friendship lit his
life and in the short time he was here
his presence brightened ours too. He
was a joy to be with.

On the morning he died he asked me to
post the enclosed letter to you.

Please accept my sincere condolences.
I will write to you again with details
of the funeral arrangements as soon as
I have them.

Yours sincerely,
Daphne Game

Senior Nurse

Raymond's mum held him tightly as he sobbed into her woollen jumper. He pulled her close and felt her tears tumble onto the back of his neck. Gently she stroked his hair and kissed his head.

After a while he turned, picked up the envelope and shook it. A smaller brown one fell on to the kitchen table. Raymond slid a finger under the flap and opened it. He felt something heavy in the bottom corner and tilted the envelope. A shiny golden key dropped into his open palm. He reached inside and pulled out a tightly folded letter, full of words from a friend who'd fallen from the world and would never return.

My dearest Raymond,

Thank you so much for your letter. It cheered me up no end. What great news about your sunflowers. We just needed to take a chance on them and with love (and the sun!) they've grown. I wish I could have seen them. Please visit next week if you can. It's perfectly all right and it'll be lovely to see you all. Please bring a photo of the flowers.

It's not too bad here. Don't worry about me. I miss home terribly, of course, but there's a wonderful nurse called Daphne who looks after us all and makes me laugh. I tell you, Raymond, if I were thirty years younger I think I'd ask her to marry me!

I've been getting around in a wheelchair, which I thought I'd hate but it's rather nice to be pushed about. People get out of the way and you always get to the front. It's amazing – rather than being old and frail I'm empowered in my chariot. Of course, when you get stuck in the mud while looking at the flowers in the garden and have to get four people to carry you back to the patio, that's a different story, and I wasn't amused. But it seemed to make EVERYONE else here laugh, so it wasn't such a bad thing.

I keep getting terrible headaches but I think it's just the after-effects of my fall. I did rather bash my head as well as my ankle, which I think has sadly had it. The doctor will keep an eye on things.

Anyway, now to important matters. You'll find in the envelope a key to my house – it's yours. I am sure I won't return there now. I've been preparing this for a little while; it was going to be a Christmas surprise. All the paperwork is in the bureau and everything has been arranged with my solicitor at Marriage's in town. My brother is none too pleased but he'll soon get over it. There shouldn't be any problem – if there is, Mr Marriage will sort it out. I suggest you get along to their offices as soon as possible and sign the paperwork though.

My home has been a happy one, with so many wonderful memories. Violet's ashes are under the white rose bush, on the left-hand side of the garden as you look from the house. Please keep her safe and, if possible, let me lie with her when my time wcomes.

You asked me in your letter if my current predicament was your fault because you'd insisted I chase my coin down the hill. Nothing is further from the truth. I may have fallen that night, but I did fly. As you get older, you'll realise how rarely those opportunities come along and how wonderful and important they are when they do.

I also need to thank you, Raymond, for three other things. You might think that I've been the older and wiser one, and that you've learnt from me (I hope I've been able to show you a thing or two though!), but actually it is I who've been given the most valuable lessons by you. Firstly, when we met, I said everything older seemed better. I wore my rose-tinted spectacles, remember? (I'm smiling now, thinking of you in *The Salt Shaker*). You've shown me that this isn't necessarily true and I'm so grateful. The future is in good hands. Secondly, I'm not scared anymore. I always worried about the things I'd miss when I'm no longer around. I was so afraid of dying but how can I miss something that I don't even know will happen? Instead, I've learned to cherish everything I've done; it's been a wonderful, eye-opening experience. I'd forgotten to live for today because I was so worried about tomorrow. You and your party story taught me that. Now I can focus on all the beautiful things in the world. I tried to get you to do that with your flowers – how could I have forgotten myself? The world really can be a wonderful place. You've opened my eyes once more.

Finally, thank you for my poem. No one has ever written anything for me before and it's truly a precious gift. It's become my heart's best treasure and rests beneath my pillow every night. I sense it lying there in the darkness and can feel the wonder of our glorious summer of sunflowers and stars.

With all my heart, thank you.

Best wishes,
Ernest – still kind and still with a dream or two up his sleeve!

CHAPTER TWENTY-FIVE

A Knock at the Door

1974

The snow was fluffy and white against the night. It swirled in gusts, building on the banks of the garden at number 43. It had been a cold winter; even February's arrival had not driven away the persistent flurries or melted the ice that piled high on the pavements.

Raymond moved towards the patio door, intending to close the curtains against the cold. He stared through the glass but saw only the glow of the electric fire and his own image reflected there. He stood back, his form bright against the darkness. He'd put on weight; his face was fuller and a stubbly black beard masked his pale skin. He smiled, secretly pleased. He held a large paintbrush up to the window and waved it, dark against his paint-splattered shirt. In the background, *Yessongs* was playing on his new stereo.

He'd been living in Ernest's old house for about a year and had decided to decorate. Finding time was the trick; his job at the DHSS left him with precious little. The clerk had been right – the social life was fantastic. He'd made lots of friends and the pub seemed a natural place to congregate after a day's work.

Ernest was never far from his thoughts and every day his friend's generosity warmed him. Ernest's brother had accepted the transfer of ownership with good grace, and with little delay Raymond had become the proud owner of Ernest's house.

The funeral had been a quiet affair. He'd travelled to Birmingham with his mum and dad. Afterwards they'd gone to Ernest's brother's house for the wake, which although sad was a wonderful celebration of Ernest's life. His old photographs were displayed in every nook and cranny, many lit by a tiny Christmas light. Raymond had stood transfixed in front of each one, in awe of Ernest's unassuming brilliance, so proud of their friendship. His excited dad had delighted in naming many of the bygone celebrities captured by Ernest's film.

A few days later, Raymond had reverently carried home a small black urn and laid Ernest's ashes under the white rosebush, next to his beloved Violet's.

That summer the blooms were large, abundant and of the purest white.

The front doorbell rang, snapping him out of his reverie, and he pulled the curtains shut with a flourish. It was late and he wanted to ignore the caller, but the bell rang again and then once more.

Raymond sighed and wandered to the front door. He opened it just a few inches.

A young woman was walking down the path, away from the house. Long black hair curled over the collar of a warm red coat. The snowflakes caught in the wool and the tangles of her hair. She turned and Raymond felt giddy as her dark, almond eyes met his.

He opened the door wider and the young woman walked back towards him.

'Excuse me,' she said. Her voice was soft, the French accent conspicuous. The words seemed almost to dance as she spoke. 'Does Mr Gardiner live here?'

'Pardon?' The music was loud and the sound of Ernest's name had thrown Raymond. He squinted and leaned forward.

'Mr Gardiner, Mr Ernest Gardiner. Does he live here?' The young woman smiled reassuringly.

'No ... I'm afraid he doesn't,' said Raymond, suspicious despite her warm manner.

'Oh ... um ...' A look of such sorrow swept over her face that Raymond felt instantly guilty. 'I am so sorry to have troubled you,' she said. She turned and began to walk down the path as quickly as the slippery ice would allow.

'Wait,' called Raymond. 'Please wait ... look, he used to live here. He was my friend ... he ... he ...' Raymond fought to find the two words he hated more than any other. 'He died.'

She turned to face him and raised her hands to her mouth, her head shaking.

'Oh no. I came here to tell him ...' She stepped backwards.

'Tell him what?'

'It doesn't matter. I must go.'

'Please tell me. I was his friend.'

She hesitated and then took a step forward.

'To tell him he has a daughter. I am his granddaughter.'

CHAPTER TWENTY-SIX

Frostbite

Raymond stood in the doorway, his mouth opening and closing wordlessly. His breath caught as if a heavy punch had slammed into his chest. He stared at the young woman until the snow-filled silence became unbearable.

Then she spoke. 'I am so sorry to have troubled you. I must be going.' She turned again and hurried away.

Raymond breathed and the cold air was like icy water, shocking him back to reality.

'Wait,' he shouted. It sounded more like an order than the plea he'd intended.

She glanced around then stumbled faster down the path.

'I must go,' she mumbled.

'Please wait. I knew Ernest. He was my friend. He gave me this house. His daughter – why didn't she contact him?' Raymond took a step into the night, his socks soaking up the snow.

The woman hesitated and turned.

'No one knew he was alive,' she said.

'But … but … please, come in. Just for ten minutes. You've come all this way for a reason; I might be able to help. Please.'

He turned and walked back into the hallway, leaving the door wide open, praying she'd follow him inside.

In a daze he made his way to the lounge. It was a muddle of paint pots, brushes, and rollers. He moved some newspapers and slumped into the familiar chair – the one he'd sat in when he'd visited Ernest – now covered with a white dust sheet. He gripped the soft arms; saw his fingers turning white with the effort.

He concentrated on the lounge door, willing it to move, his ears straining over his pounding heart to hear the hoped-for footsteps.

There was no sound and the cold air from the open front door began to filter through the room. Raymond shivered, only in part because of the cold. She wasn't coming. He leapt up and ran into the hallway, knocking over a paint pot in his haste.

It was eerily quiet. The front door was still wide open and the moonlight lit the room with a translucent glow. Ice had formed on the carpet by the door where the snowflakes had blown inside and melted.

'Damn it,' he whispered.

He dived into the night, dressed in just a T-shirt, jeans and socks. The cold air hit him a hammer blow and he reeled backwards, gasping for breath. The young woman was nowhere to be seen. He reached the end of the garden path and looked left and right. Still no trace. The heavy flurries of snow had covered any footprints. He chose left and skidded along the street on his frozen stockinged feet. At the end of the road he looked both ways but she had gone.

'Shit,' he cursed quietly, holding his head in his freezing hands.

He retraced his steps and continued along the road, past his house, in the opposite direction. He shivered violently and wondered whether his numb feet were at risk of frostbite.

Thinking he'd lost her and about to give up, he turned a corner. There, twenty yards ahead of him, was the woman. She trudged slowly into the night, huddled against the cold, her long hair lit by moonlight and speckled with white snowflakes. She reached a small yellow car and opened the driver's door.

Raymond gasped. 'Wait ... please wait.' It was difficult to talk; his jaw was tight and his teeth chattered.

She stopped, hesitated and turned holding the car door open. She looked at Raymond and raised a hand to her mouth.

'Please, you must talk to me. I was Ernest's friend. He told me all kinds of stories but never mentioned a daughter.'

The woman smiled, her eyes darting from his desperate face to his sodden feet. 'You must get indoors. You will freeze out here. Where are your shoes?'

'I don't know. I don't care. It was just so important I see you and I couldn't waste a second.'

'I-I don't think Ernest knew he had a daughter,' she said. 'His friend in France – Mirabelle – she was my grandmother.'

'What? Wait … no … that's not right. Mira died in a bombing. Ernest was heartbroken.'

'No, she didn't die. She lived a long and wonderful life. She kept a journal, which I have been reading since I was a little girl. That's how I know about Monsieur Gardiner.' She shook her head. 'I am sorry – I really have to go.'

'Please, t-there's a pub down the road. It's called The Quiet Life. C-can you meet me there tomorrow night about 8 o'clock? I've got work during the day. You can see how important it is – look at me. I'm half-dead with the c-cold.'

'I don't know. I have a lot to do. I go back to France the day after tomorrow.'

'Please, you came all this way. Just take a chance. Everything happens for a reason.'

She laughed then, a gleeful birdsong in the winter wilderness. She turned and faced him through the snow. 'Those words are in my grandmother's journal. Bill said them.'

Her smiling eyes found his and Raymond felt a warmth filling his body, keeping him safe from the cold.

'Yes … yes … you see, I know loads,' said Raymond. 'I know the story, everything. But … but … it's all wrong.' The words tumbled from him and his hands gesticulated wildly. 'I need to know what really happened. I—' He sighed and rested his hands by his side. He could do no more. 'Please,' he whispered.

The woman smiled again and began to get into the car. Raymond took a step forward then looked down at himself. The situation was ridiculous; she must think him mad, shivering in front of her, shoeless and in just a T-shirt and jeans.

He lowered his head. Enough.

'The Quiet Life at 8 o'clock. I will see you then.' She curled into the driver's seat, closed the door, and shouted a muffled *au revoir*.

The car pulled away slowly, sliding a little on the frozen road. Its rear lights glowed, two warm red embers disappearing into the night.

Raymond skipped back through the slush to his house. He was no longer cold.

CHAPTER TWENTY-SEVEN
The Quiet Life

The next day dragged. Raymond couldn't focus on his work and several colleagues asked if he was all right. Nothing seemed real and although the sun shone brightly, and the snow was slowly thawing, everything appeared grey and on hold. It was as if he were waiting in the foyer for a long-awaited and favourite show to start. At four, he flexed off work and caught the bus home.

He moped around the house. He wasn't in the mood for painting so he flicked between the three TV channels. Nothing sparked his interest.

At seven he showered. By seven thirty he was on the way to The Quiet Life.

It was still bitterly cold. The snow had melted during the day but the slush had turned to ice and he took great care as he walked along the treacherous paths. The roads were now quite clear and Raymond made the most of a car-less evening.

The Quiet Life was its usual welcoming self. The subdued yellow glow and the fading floral sofas around the wall gave the pub a homely feel. At the bar, regulars sat on their high stools, listening dutifully to the landlord's stories. Raymond squeezed between them and ordered a pint of lager in a mug. A brand-new glass cabinet full of pasties caught his eye so he decided to try one and he took it over to the corner by the window where he'd sat with Ernest. Since that time he'd become a regular, often meeting friends from work, though whenever he visited he thought back to that night when he'd flown down the slope.

From his seat he could see the bar and the door. A low hubbub of chatter filled the smoky air. Older regulars, their stomachs straining their shirt buttons, talked mainly in twos or threes. A larger group of youngsters occupied the opposite corner, and Raymond suspected that several were under eighteen. They supped their half pints sheepishly, talking quietly about last weekend's football results. In the public bar a game of pool was in progress and the clatter of balls and raucous laughter interrupted the calm of the saloon.

Time seemed to stand still. He bit into his pasty. The flaky pastry caught in his throat and he helped it down with a mouthful of beer.

He stared at the clock and waited.

The anticipation was unbearable. The previous evening had been a shock; first the young woman, then the news of Mira. He wished with all his heart that Ernest was sitting with him and tried to think of the questions his friend would have asked.

He looked at the clock. Eight fifteen. Icy panic cut into his spine and tickled the tips of his fingers.

Where was she? Had she changed her mind?

He surveyed the room.

Maybe she'd already arrived. Gone to the public bar. Gone home when she couldn't find him.

He stood quickly, banging his thighs against the table and sending it scraping across the floor. Several people looked around and, embarrassed, he slumped back into his seat, unsure what to do.

Look outside? Go to the public bar? Leave?

The turmoil made him giddy.

He took another sip of lager. It was now BFL, as his friends would say – below flob level. He smiled and looked at the clock again. It seemed the faster his heart beat the slower time went.

The pub door opened and all heads turned. The excitement sent Raymond's pulse racing. He breathed in a deep ocean of air. His spirits buoyed then sunk, as he realised the young woman was not one of the new arrivals. A middle-aged couple stamped their feet on the mat and nodded to several regulars. An icy blast of wind accompanied them, sending an involuntary shudder through the room. White smudges on the couple's coats revealed that snow had begun to fall again.

Time dragged unmoving, but that was how he wished it now; the later it got the less likely the chance of her arrival. He looked around the bar. Where was she? He had so many questions.

He watched the group of youngsters laugh and relax as

the beer mellowed their nerves. They had their whole lives ahead of them, but he knew how easy it was to drift; he'd done a lot of that.

When Ernest had died, Raymond vowed he'd write a book by the time he was thirty. Over a year had flown by and he'd not written a single word. He imagined his life as a silk ribbon stretching ahead of him, twisting and turning, but with every second that passed the silk became a little shorter. He shook his head and looked at the clock. Eight thirty. His ribbon had shortened by fifteen minutes and he'd not even noticed.

And then it hit him. She wasn't coming.

Why would she? Who would meet a complete stranger in a pub? He'd been a total idiot to think she would.

He stood and pulled on his coat. His limbs felt heavy with sadness, and a weariness overcame him. He turned and stepped towards the door. It flew open in a flurry of snow.

She whooshed into the bar. Olive skin, long dark hair floating behind her. She seemed startled, as if the lights of The Quiet Life had temporarily blinded her, and she moved her head quickly from side to side, searching.

She didn't see him and hurried towards the public bar, holding a battered brown briefcase that swung precariously close to the glass-laden tables.

Raymond stood transfixed, watching her enter, then return to the saloon, her eyes all the while seeking something. Then she found him, and the biggest of beaming smiles lit her face. She walked quickly, dropped the briefcase, clasped his warm hand between her frozen ones and squeezed.

'I am so sorry.' Her words were rushed, and she breathed as if to steady herself. 'My hire car wouldn't start and I had to get a taxi. I was sure you would be gone.' She seemed about to hug him but just smiled again. 'But you are still here. Thank you for waiting.'

Raymond was speechless. He could only look at her, his mouth slightly open.

She was beautiful.

The golden glow of the lights gently illuminated her face. Her big brown eyes, edged with black eyeliner, were expectant and questioning. With a brush of her hand she swept a curl of hair away from her cheek, but almost instantly it fell back into place.

Raymond self-consciously looked around the room. The group of youths and the regulars at the bar were staring, intrigued by this strange meeting.

'Let me get you a drink,' he said.

'Red wine, merci.' She sat down on the sofa.

Raymond walked to the bar and felt the eyes of the regulars following him. He imagined them wondering how he knew this beautiful woman, and he stood a little taller and smiled as he ordered the drinks and returned to his seat.

'I am so sorry,' she said again. 'Thank you.'

'It's okay. I'm just glad you're here. I was so worried. I couldn't contact you and thought I'd never see you again. I have so many questions.' He looked around the pub; most people had now returned to their own lives and conversations. 'I'm Ray by the way.' He extended his hand.

The woman took it again and held it in hers.

'Ah, Ray, like the sun. That's lovely. My name is Aimee.'

'Oh, Aimee ... like ... er ... um.' Raymond felt the heat rush to his cheeks.

Aimee laughed, a wonderful, joyous childlike giggle that made Raymond feel instantly at ease.

'Um ... so are you staying in England long?' He tried to appear casual, not wanting to mention Mira too soon although he was desperate for information.

'No, I have been here for three days. I go back to France tomorrow.'

'Tomorrow? Have you enjoyed your stay?'

'It has been cold, much colder than France. I should have waited until the summer but I was impatient.' She looked at Raymond and smiled, as if inviting him to enquire further, but he remained resolute.

'Have you visited anywhere else?' he asked nonchalantly.

'Yes, before I came to the UK, I took a trip to Bailleul.'

He could no longer contain himself. 'Bailleul!' he replied somewhat louder than he'd intended, and several people turned to look over. He spoke again, more quietly this time. 'Bailleul. Where Ernest and Bill met Mira?'

'Yes. Mirabelle was my grandmother. She was a remarkable woman and lived an extraordinary life. With her husband she travelled all over the world, raising money for charities that were close to her heart. My grandfather was a musician. He played with the Berlin Philharmonic Orchestra.'

Aimee could barely keep still. A smile flashed across her face, lighting the gloomy corner, her pride unmistakable.

'They were always together. When he was playing in

the orchestra, she was out persuading people to give her money or go to the charity concerts her husband had arranged. They were quite a force.' She laughed.

'But Ernest was sure she'd died when her farmhouse was bombed.' The words gushed out of him, his dam of indifference breached in a second. 'He saw her body,' he added, as if more proof were needed.

'Well, it wasn't my grandmother's. She spoke of a young English photographer who spent a wonderful summer with her in Bailleul before he was killed.'

'But ... but he wasn't killed!' said Raymond. He paused to catch his breath. 'How do you know all this?'

Mira leant closer and Raymond mirrored her movement, conspirators huddled over the table.

'When I was a little girl,' Aimee continued quietly, 'I sat on my grandmother's knee while she read to me from an old green journal. I loved hearing about the countryside; it was a different world to the city I was used to. I looked forward to those days, and the journal became something magical. But she would never finish it, despite my protests, and we would always start the book again from the beginning. As I grew older I visited her less and less, and those days, snuggled in her lap, listening to her adventures, came to an end.' Mira sighed and looked sad. 'My grandmother died six years ago, and when my mother was clearing her house, she discovered an old wooden chest. It was full of memorabilia and she gave it to me to look through. At the bottom of the chest I found the green journal. Imagine how I felt. I could hardly breathe. I began to turn the pages my grandmother would never read. It was a harrowing tale and I can understand why she didn't want to burden me with it. That is where I discovered Ernest Gardiner – a young English photographer – and his friend Bill. Since then I've been researching the story. It's been nearly five years and I've probably written a hundred letters.' She laughed again. 'I found out there were only sixteen official British photographers in the First World War. So I wrote to the Ministry of Defence, asking for service records, and to my surprise I discovered that Ernest Gardiner had left the army, alive and well. He'd also lived in the same house for over fifty years, so it wasn't hard to find him.' She looked at Raymond and whispered sadly, 'Just a little too late, it seems.'

She reached down to the floor and lifted the battered brown briefcase on to the table.

'Anyway, look what I have with me.'

She opened the scratched clasp, then removed an olive-green notebook and laid it on the table. Dirt had accumulated along the edges of the dog-eared cover, leaving a line of black smudges. There was a look of great age about it.

Aimee smiled at Raymond, a secret and excited smile, then opened the briefcase wider and took out a slim black box about nine inches long and four inches high. It too was old and there were dents and scratches all over it. Raymond looked closer. Scorch marks fanned the side.

Aimee clicked a tiny button and the front of the box swung open. She reached inside and gently pulled. A small camera appeared, its dry black leather bellows expanding concertina-like behind it.

'It's a No. 1 Autographic Kodak Junior. I've researched it,' she said, looking pleased with herself. 'I think it was Ernest's. I wanted to return it to him.' She watched him as he processed her words.

'What? No … you're joking.' Raymond couldn't stop himself – he picked up the camera, turning it in his hand with reverence. 'But where did you get it? How do you know?'

'My grandmother, Mira, mentioned it in her journals. There are also these photographs that she developed after the war.' Aimee reached into the briefcase and took out a small photo album. 'There are only two pictures, I'm afraid, but this keeps them safe.' She opened the cover and passed the album to Raymond.

The pictures were just a few inches tall and wide. They were black and white, and time had left them faded, especially around the edges. The first showed a young woman with long dark hair like Aimee's, looking sadly at the camera. Her mouth curved gently into the tiniest of smiles. Flowers bloomed behind her, and hooked over her shoulder was a wicker basket full of freshly cut sunflowers. Raymond looked up from the picture and mouthed, *Mira?*

She nodded.

He looked at the second picture and his eyes widened in recognition. A boy in a uniform smiled up through the creases of the faded photograph. The pictured was skewed at an odd angle, as if something had jogged the camera at the moment of the shutter's release. Still, without a shadow of doubt it was Ernest. He stared back across the years, his eyes alive, delighted and innocent.

Raymond's fingers trembled as they gently caressed the picture.

'I can't believe it. It's Ernest. It's bloody Ernest!' said Raymond, laughing. 'Sorry I didn't mean to ...' He half-stood, barely able to stop himself from leaping. 'But ... this ... oh, goodness ... but how do you know Mira's daughter was Ernest's?'

'Let me read the journal to you,' said Aimee, trying to hide her own excitement. 'I marked the pages this afternoon.'

Raymond sat back down and leaned closer. He could smell the journal's musky scent. It was beginning to fall apart, and some of the pages stuck stubbornly together, but Aimee persevered and, at last, she spread the journal open on the table at the place she wanted.

The neat copperplate handwriting surprised Raymond. The words flowed like perfect waves across the page, each sentence finishing with a looping flourish.

Aimee began to translate.

CHAPTER TWENTY-EIGHT
The Journal

This evening, two Tommies arrived at the
house. They will be staying with us for a while.
I had been sitting and reading the poetry book
father bought for me but had lost interest and
was thinking about the war and father, and
staring at the night sky and the stars when I
heard the door creak.

Peering through the crack I saw a boy in
an oversized uniform. I beckoned him in and
asked him to sit with me. He was embarrassed;
I could see his cheeks turning red. I decided
to be cruel and make things worse, so I took
his hand in mine and stared at him. All to no
avail – he refused to look at me. I recognised
him as one of the men who had waved to us
from their lorry as we washed our clothes in the
river. He seemed so different. In the lorry, with

his companions he was full of confidence and bravado, but now I could see he was young and innocent. I asked if his friend was here too but the boy would not talk save only to say that his name was Ernest Gardiner. Then he continued to stare into space. I told him I was troubled about father and as I spoke he turned his head towards me, concerned and worried for me despite all that was happening in his own life. I felt ashamed of my games, but I offended him again when I said that one so young should not see these horrors. In an instant he said more words than during the whole of our meeting, declaring he was not young at all – nearly eighteen! I struggled to keep my laughter inside and had to look away from him into the night. Luckily, at that moment, a shooting star shot across the sky and I was able to distract him. He asked me about my poetry book and wanted me to read to him. It was my turn to feel embarrassed as I read William Wordsworth in my poor English to a well-spoken Englishman, but I did it. And when I finished the words moved me and I felt very sad. I held his hand again, not to mock him but because in that moment I needed to feel a human touch to chase away my loneliness.

The back door opened and the boy's friend appeared. I have never seen anyone move so quickly and the boy pulled his hand from mine

*as if he had placed it in a pot of boiling water!
He went red as a beetroot and stuttered a
hello to his friend. Once again it took all my
willpower to stop myself from laughing. To my
surprise, his friend can speak very good French.
His name is Bill and he is certainly how I
have imagined a soldier would be – rugged and
strong – but he is also very funny and he teases
the boy.*

*I took the two of them into the kitchen
and gave them cheese, bread and wine. By
then I was feeling very sleepy, and I bade the
men good night and left them to their snacks.
As I turned my back to leave, I could see the
older soldier reflected in the kitchen window,
making a voluptuous shape with his hands and
laughing at his young friend, who was shaking
his head. Rather than making me feel cross,
it was nice to be the centre of attention. And
for the first time in a long while I felt some
happiness and a little bit of hope return to the
world.*

Raymond shook his head. 'I don't know what to say. It's
… it's … goodness. Ernest told me all about when he first
met Mira. It was a beautiful evening and he never forgot
it. That poem by William Wordsworth – I can't remember
which one – but it was always his favourite.'

'There's more. Listen.' Aimee turned the pages until she
reached her next marker near the end of the journal. She

swallowed a mouthful of wine and began to read again. Raymond tried his hardest to keep his eyes on the book but he couldn't resist looking at Aimee. To his embarrassment, she occasionally caught his secret glances when, without warning, she looked up and fleetingly met his gaze with a smile.

My summer continues and I am so grateful that my two friends have come to stay with us. It is as though the war is somewhere else, far far away. The weather today has been glorious. The heat is intense and the sun seems to spend the whole day high in the sky. There is rarely any shade but it is perfect, though I am sure Ernest finds it difficult with his pale skin.

Yet again, we spent the day by the river, dipping our feet into the cooling water, the boys sitting shirtless, and me a floozie, my dress high over my thighs and pulled down exposing my shoulders. If anyone could see me I am sure they'd be shocked by my behaviour but I am alive and who knows when I may not be. I am getting to know the boys better each day. Bill is confident, brash and gregarious. He has a joke for every occasion, but he cares deeply for Ernest despite his constant teasing. He tells us about his dreams and how he will involve us in his restaurant when the war is over. There is always a glint of hope when he speaks and I can see Ernest staring ahead into the distance, as I often do, lost in thought, thinking of the future. Bill's favourite saying is 'Everything happens for a reason'. Ernest and I can almost predict when he will say it and we mimic him each time. It is funny and Ernest's chance for revenge.

Ernest is quiet and kind and shy. He always wears a small camera around his neck and takes endless photographs of us, winding the handle noisily after every shot. He is probably ten years younger than Bill and me and he seems so innocent, little more than a boy in a man's world. But when I look into his wonderful blue eyes, I see something deep and unfathomable that tempts me to dive in and discover what lies within. Bill took me aside last night and quietly warned me that Ernest is falling in love with me. He asked me to be careful, for I will surely break the boy's heart. I laughed it off but I know it to be true. I see Ernest's secret sideways glances, the way he hangs on my every word, and when I look at him he struggles to meet my gaze. My worst behaviour has been to clasp his hand in mine at every opportunity and to watch his cheeks slowly turn red, despite his sunburn! But as the days have gone by I have discovered that it has been nice to feel his fingers or to link arms with him as we walk home, despite Bill's tiny head shakes of reprimand, which I bat back with an innocent smile.

Aimee paused and looked at Raymond. 'If you want another drink, I'd better get it. The next bit is rather long and, well, you'll probably need a drink by the end of it. What would you like?' she said.

'Just a pint of lager, please,' said Raymond. 'But I can—'

But Aimee was already out of her seat and on her way to the bar, heads following her as she went.

Raymond marvelled at the journal. He ran his fingers over the fragile brown pages, trying to feel their history and move back the years to when Ernest was a boy and in love with this wonderful woman, whose words sung from another time. He closed his eyes and lay his hand flat on the paper, wishing that world into existence.

Aimee coughed.

'Oh sorry,' said Raymond, embarrassed. 'I was just trying to imagine what it was like. It's amazing that Mira held this book all those years ago.'

'I know. And don't worry – it has the same effect on me,' said Aimee. 'The next bit is sad. It's right at the end of the journal. Look at this page first though. It just has one line.' Aimee went to another of her markers.

Today I heard my father died. My life has ended.

'It doesn't look as if she wrote in her journal for a while after that,' said Aimee, 'and then she went back and filled in the days she'd missed. It sounds as if her world had been turned upside down. It was terrible. Listen.'

*I have not written for over a week. How can
the world change in such a short space of time?
From being so happy I am now at my lowest
ebb; I am in hell. My mother, father and young
Ernest have all been killed. I have no idea
where Bill is. He has almost certainly met the
same fate. My heart is broken. There are no
more tears left to cry. I have been living in the
woods near the farmhouse, and have managed
to scavenge some food from abandoned houses.
Luckily it is still warm and I have been able
to sleep with only a covering of branches and
leaves. All is devastation here. The bombing
went on and on for days, then soldiers
swarmed about the countryside, advancing and
retreating. I hid in a badger sett, covered with
mud, and watched the battles. Sometimes the
soldiers have been so close I could have untied
their boot laces. I dread to think what will
happen if I am discovered.*

*I think the Germans have taken over the
town as the bombing has now stopped and
there has been no further advance since the
last one a couple of days ago. All is chaos
and destruction. I have been sleeping when I
can during the day and scavenging at night.
I am filthy and live like the pigs we kept on
the farm, but the mud is my protector. The
only comfort I have is this journal. It is the
last reminder of the farmhouse and I can look*

back over the pages to happier times. I keep it sheltered in a hollow tree together with Ernest's camera. I hope perhaps it will be found one day when this war is over. Then a little piece of me will remain in the world. I think my own chances of survival are very small.

I have not felt like writing until today. So much has happened and my mind has been broken, but this morning the sun was shining through the trees and it looked so beautiful. So I thought I would try again only to find that my pencil, like me, is in a sorry state. I will write as much as I can before the lead breaks again.

On the day I heard my father died we had awoken to a loud knocking on the front door. The horrible soldier who had been so rude to Mother escorted Ernest and Bill into town. They had to go to the square to take photographs of the general on his new horse, something they had been joking about for days but had hoped would never happen. I had breakfast and did my chores, then walked into the town. It was quiet in the normally bustling streets but in the square it was chaos. Soldiers lined every side, three or four deep. I tried to see what was going on, but it was impossible, even standing on tiptoe. I seemed invisible to the men, who ignored my feeble attempts to

get to the front. Eventually I spied a statue;
remarkably, the large plinth on which it stood
was empty and I climbed on top. Over the
soldiers' heads I could see the general wearing
a bright-red uniform, sitting astride a large,
frightened chestnut mare. Its forelegs were
pacing up and down and it seemed about to
bolt at any moment. The groom was frantically
holding the bridle, trying to keep it still, while
the general, who was certainly no horseman,
sat precariously in the saddle. His face was as
red as his uniform and the sun glinted on the
sweat that dripped from his chin. I then saw
Ernest and Bill and my heart melted. They both
looked so small in that huge square, surrounded
by the baying crowd. I was so proud of them.
They were performers on a stage. Ernest was
looking through his camera, which he had set
up on a tripod, and Bill was speaking to the
general. Suddenly the crowd were counting
in unison – two, three. The chant became
louder, almost deafening, and I could see that
the horse, her ears pricked backwards, was
beginning to panic. Four, five. There was a
flash and a puff of smoke from the camera as
Ernest took his picture. The horse bolted. How
the general did not fall off instantly I will
never know, but he was able to grab the horse
around the neck and remain in the saddle as it
raced round the square, boxed in by the soldiers,

who were waving and shouting and making
the whole situation worse. Finally, the general
slid off the horse and his men raced to lift him
to his feet. I could hear angry shouting but
couldn't make out the words. And then I saw
Bill leave hurriedly. Eventually the general
seemed to calm down and stood in different
positions, letting Ernest take some more
pictures of him, which seemed to cause even
more merriment amongst the men. Finally, the
general grew tired of the poses and pushed his
way through the crowds, which immediately
dispersed.

I watched Ernest pack away his equipment
and I couldn't help but smile. His uniform
was undoubtedly too big, and he seemed so
young, yet he had commanded the arena. I felt
so happy and proud that he was my friend.
I climbed down from the plinth and walked
towards him. He was busy with his boxes
but something made him look up. And when
he saw me, his smile was enough to warm me
in the coldest of winters. It was so radiant
that I had to look away. As I did, I noticed a
battered old franc, half-buried in the ground.
I picked it up, skipped over to Ernest and
gave it to him for good luck. He then made me
stand in front of him and the few soldiers who
remained while he took a photograph of me. I
was self-conscious and embarrassed but I felt

like a movie star and I laughed as he clicked
the shutter.

We walked back to the farmhouse with Bill,
who had been given latrine duty. Ernest and
I found that very funny. I think Bill wanted
revenge on Ernest for escaping any punishment
and he spent the walk home flirting with me.
I am ashamed to say that I joined in with the
teasing even though I knew how Ernest felt,
and I ran ahead, hand in hand with Bill, leaving
poor Ernest to carry his heavy camera and glass
plates. We reached the farmhouse with Ernest
lagging far behind and out of sight. My mother
met us at the gate. She was in a terrible state,
crying uncontrollably. She gave me a letter that
told me father had been killed. As I read it, I felt
myself getting hotter. Coloured patches began to
obscure my vision. Suddenly I found myself in
Bill's arms, my legs having given way beneath
me. I was quietly sobbing on to his shoulder
when Ernest arrived. I realise now the poor boy
thought we were in an amorous embrace but I
had no stomach to explain myself or comfort him
and I rushed into the house.

That evening I stared out of the window
at the stars. Nothing would ever be the
same again. All was sombre and still aside
from my mother's muffled sobs and the boys'
soft whispers, their heads close together in
conversation, both unable to look at me.

Bill left for his latrine duty and Ernest followed him out of the room. I heard him climbing the stairs to his bedroom. After a while I couldn't bear the sound of my mother's tears any longer. I kissed her goodnight and made my way to bed. I pulled the blankets tightly around me and snuggled into my feather pillows. I was exhausted by my grief and could hardly keep my eyes open, but sleep would not come. Images of my father lying dead and lonely in a muddy field circled endlessly in my mind. Then I thought of Ernest, so young and so likely to be killed. Had he ever been loved or felt the joy and closeness of another's touch?

When this journal is found, I am sure I will be dead, otherwise I would not have the courage to write these words. But I want the truth to be in the world, scandalous as it is.

I saw Ernest, young, alone and frightened, with his dazzling blue eyes, always smiling. And I wanted him to experience the intensity of love before it was too late. My passion would be my gift to him. Not one bone in my body will ever regret what I did and in the end my gift that night was Ernest's last.

Looking back now, in the cold light of morning, I can see my father's death had broken me. I wanted Ernest to be happy but I, too, longed to feel alive again, to be held. I would have done anything to wring the last pieces of life out of that barren and bleak world we then found ourselves in.

I crept into his room, took off my nightshirt and seduced him. I put his shy hands on me and guided him. And for those moments life and love came back to me. We fell asleep in each other's arms until I was woken by Bill's gentle touch on my back. I turned to find him smiling. He raised a finger to his lips and mouthed the words – Your mother will be up soon. I knew she mustn't see me in the boy's bedroom. She had suffered enough already without thinking her daughter was a harlot. I crept out of the bed and looked at Ernest, peaceful in the half-light of sunrise. He still wore a small smile on his beautiful young face and his eyelids fluttered in a far-off dream. 'Thank you,' whispered Bill. 'You're wonderful.' And then he hugged me and kissed me softly on the cheek.

Raymond sat quietly, slowly digesting the information; he couldn't bring himself to look at Aimee.

'Ernest told me about the night Mira came to his room and ...' Suddenly everything clicked into place. 'So that was when she ...?'

Aimee nodded.

'There was no one else in Mira's life, so the baby must have been Ernest's.' Aimee looked at Raymond. 'Listen – there is a little more.'

Aimee turned to the end of the journal.

I have not written in my journal for a few days but my life has not changed. Food is becoming harder to find, and it is certainly getting colder at night. I am still the mud queen and can now feel the lice crawling inside my clothes. I live like a wild animal and each minute that I survive is both a success and a torment. Every day I become weaker; I can hardly hold my pencil, which is becoming smaller and smaller as I try unsuccessfully to sharpen it. The journal has been my rock. I still look back over the pages; they remind me that life was once good and can surely be good again. I am determined that this journal must tell my story so I will carry on, one word at a time. I pray that one day a young beautiful woman, warm and safe, her hair brushed and tied, will read my words. Not because I want pity or because I want her to appreciate her lot but because I will know that this hell has ended and that sense and beauty and laughter have returned to the world.

These next words will be the hardest to write. That last day is still a blur to me even though flashes of memory insist on flitting around my head as I sleep. I remember bringing the boys coffee and bread as they sat on the wooden bench in the front garden. I was still sad, of course, and thoughts of my father would not leave me, but the morning was beautiful and the garden bright with blooms. I cut some sunflowers and lay the stems one on top of the other in my wicker basket. Ernest was in a daze. I think he half-thought he'd dreamt the previous evening, and that made me smile despite everything. He took a photograph of me posing with my basket. Then I went inside to put the flowers in water. My mother was in the kitchen; she took the basket from me and said she would arrange them. I kissed her and went into the back garden with my journal. I needed to be alone with my thoughts and to remember my father.

It was a beautiful and peaceful morning. I closed my eyes and tilted my head towards the sun, feeling it warm my face. There was not a sound save the breeze and muffled laughter from the front of the house. Then in an instant I was lifted into the air and thrown across the garden in a maelstrom of glass and wood. I must have passed out because when I woke I could see flames flickering from the windows of the farmhouse. I was covered in dirt and my arm was awkwardly pinned behind me. I sat up and to my relief found I could move my arms and legs. I began to half-crawl, half-stagger towards the farmhouse, trying unsuccessfully to stifle my hopeless sobs. It was like moving through deep water; each inch took every bit of my willpower. As I reached the back door, something burst inside me and every sound

ever made exploded in my head. I stumbled
backwards as the magnitude of the situation
sunk in. There were explosions everywhere.
Rockets were hissing overhead but worst of all I
could hear the farmhouse crackling and burning,
turning my childhood to ashes. I pushed the
door open and stumbled inside. Those rooms, so
familiar throughout my life, were now hard to
recognise as they filled with smoke and debris.
Ahead of me the stairwell had collapsed and I
clambered over the rubble and into the kitchen.
I saw my wicker basket first, then my mother's
tiny hand still clutching the handle, her legs
bloodied and bent beneath her. She was buried
under huge slabs of concrete and wood, and the
floor was awash with dark-red blood. I fell to
my knees and tried to scrape the bricks off her
body but there were too many and every time I
removed one, another would slip into its place.
I sat and sobbed uncontrollably. Then as I put
my hand down on the floor to lever myself up,
I touched something soft and leathery. I picked
it up and held it close to my face to better see
what it was. Through the smoke I made out
Ernest's camera case. I scrambled around in a
blind panic and soon found his camera. With
horror I touched Ernest's cold hand and saw
his leg bent and twisted at an impossible angle.
I could do nothing but scream but even that
animal sorrow was taken away from me as

more mortars slammed into the house, greedily drowning every sound with their own. I ran, colliding into walls and tripping over fallen beams. How I found my way through the house I will never know but I did, and I crashed through the door into the back garden, retching into the summer air. Explosions continued to shake the ground and once outside I didn't stop running until I reached the woods, where I collapsed face down in the mud, gasping for breath, choking like a drowning fish. I do not know how long I lay there but when eventually the bombardment ceased, I eased myself up and rested forlornly against a tree. I looked down – I still held Ernest's camera tightly – my fingers were white and numb with the effort. And in my apron pocket was my journal.

I returned to the farmhouse a couple of days later but it was a blackened pile of rubble. I searched the gardens for Bill but there was no sign of him.

Over the past week I have wondered why Bill thanked me that night, but as I write these words it is clear – he loved Ernest. He loved him as much as I did. He always looked after him, wanted the best for him, wanted him to experience all that life offered. I know now that he must have followed his young friend into the farmhouse and perished with him in the flames.

Raymond looked at Aimee. He felt a strange mixture of excitement and sadness.

'So the photographs are from that camera?' he asked, nodding towards the black box on the table.

'Yes. After the war my grandmother discovered the undeveloped film still in the camera. She got it processed and these,' – Aimee pointed to the photo album – 'were the only two photographs on the roll.'

Raymond sighed and shook his head in disbelief and wonder. He picked up the album.

'That's incredible,' he said quietly. 'Just think …' He looked more closely at the first picture, marvelling at Mira and Aimee's likeness. He wondered how many sunflowers must have grown in that garden and how feeble his own attempts to cultivate them had been. Despite Mira's tiny smile, there was a sadness about the picture. Then he remembered the news of her father's death the day before.

His eyes moved to the second photograph. He tilted the page so Ernest stood upright. There was no mistaking his proud, beaming smile of accomplishment, and Raymond couldn't help from smiling with him. The beer was working its magic, and he mellowed at the sight of his old friend, then so young, at the start of his life.

He sighed. 'Things change so fast. In this picture Ernest looks so happy, but the farmhouse must have been bombed soon after it was taken.'

'Yes,' whispered Aimee.

'And Mira was so right about Bill,' said Raymond. 'Ernest told me they were both knocked off their feet by the first blast but Bill got up and raced into the farmhouse to rescue Mira. He did it without a thought for his own safety and told Ernest to stay where he was. Ernest said there were more explosions, and he was sent flying into a tree. When he woke and went back to the farmhouse, he discovered Bill's body next to Mira's. She was still clutching the wicker basket.'

'But it was Mira's mother,' said Aimee quietly.

'God.' And then realising what he'd said, Raymond quickly whispered, 'Sorry, Lord.'

They sat in silence for a while. He felt helpless, wishing the world were different.

'But what would have happened if they'd known?'

'I've been thinking about that too, ever since I found out that Ernest didn't die in the farmhouse. So many lives would be different now. For a start, I might not have been born. My mother would have lived a completely different life.'

'Oh, yes … Goodness, I didn't even think of that,' said Raymond.

'And, actually, Mira had an amazing life. She and Ernest were so different in age and cultures – who knows what might have happened?'

'I know, and Ernest had a wonderful life too. He was happily married for fifty years. But, oh, I so wish he'd known,' said Raymond.

'Me too.' Aimee smiled. 'Let me read the last two entries.'

I am on my last page. There is little left of my pencil or myself, and each individual letter, let alone word, has become a titanic act of will. I have not eaten for days. I am sure I have only stayed alive this long by licking the dew from the leaves each morning. My father always said to never give up. It was our family motto and I haven't. I am sure we will get through this and the world will become better, but I am too tired now. I think the time has come for me to lie still and wait for sleep to take me to a happier place. If you read this, please don't think badly of me. I tried

Raymond felt tears well heavy behind his eyelids. He looked down and concentrated on the journal, swallowing hard. Aimee continued.

I may not survive but there is hope. A young German soldier found me lying in my badger's hole. I was delirious but conscious enough to know this was the end and I prepared myself for some final, hideous torture before death. Instead, I felt him lift me gently. He dripped water between my parched lips, then took bread from his bag and broke it into tiny pieces and fed me as if I were the most precious person on the planet. His name is Oscar. He says he will return tomorrow and

Aimee gently closed the book. 'That's all there is. Mira didn't keep another journal.'

'But …' Raymond looked down at the closed cover. 'But there must be.'

'My grandfather, Oscar, came back to France after the war. He found Mirabelle living at a cousin's house with her little girl, my mother. He told everyone that the girl was his. You can imagine … an illegitimate child in those days would have been frowned upon. He took them back to Germany, where he played violin in the Berlin Philharmonic Orchestra. They travelled all over the world and eventually settled in France. They lived a very happy life.' Aimee sipped wine. She looked thoughtful, as if she needed to explain something.

'My grandfather said that in the war he'd been saved by a young British soldier who'd thrown him across a trench just before a rocket exploded where he'd been standing. The soldier saved his life and he thought it honourable and fair that he should now help the child of a British soldier. He never did this begrudgingly, nor was he ever resentful. It was as it should be, he said. And my mother would often say that he was the most marvellous father anyone could have ever wished for.'

Raymond rose half out of his seat. 'You … you won't believe this.' And then to Ernest he whispered, 'Everything happens for a reason.'

'Pardon?'

'Oh nothing. It's just that Ernest told me he'd rescued a German soldier once. And then the German soldier saved him. Wouldn't it be amazing if that man was your grandfather?'

Raymond and Aimee held each other's gaze, their

smiles widening as the thought nestled and grew.

'How do you know for sure that Ernest had a daughter?' Raymond asked.

She laughed. 'Ah, well, this is the skeleton in our family closet. I am sure all families have at least one. I don't think my mother wanted to tell me and she'd have been quite happy if the secret had remained buried by the years. But once I'd read the journal and started doing some research, she could see how interested I was. One day she sat me down and said she had something to tell me. I wondered what on earth it was going to be, but that afternoon she told me Mira's story. She painted a far more romantic picture of events though. She hadn't read the journal!' Aimee giggled, a wonderful joyous sound that warmed Raymond. 'Mirabelle and Oscar told her that same story when she was eighteen.'

'So your mum knew that Ernest was her real father.'

'Yes, but she thought him dead. And in any case, Oscar had raised my mother as his own and in her eyes he was always her real dad … and my wonderful grandfather, of course.' Aimee laughed again. 'My mother was so shocked when she found out that Ernest was alive. She didn't know what to do with herself and I am sure she'd have preferred things to end there. But when she realised how determined I was to visit, she gave me her blessing, even though she didn't want to come with me.'

They sat in silence, sipping their drinks as if the world around them no longer existed. Cosy in the corner, the alcohol warming them, their thoughts soared. All those possibilities, dead-ends and new beginnings.

Did everything really happen for a reason?

Raymond found it difficult to remember the twists and turns of the last hour. He wanted to run his fingers over the journal, hold the photographs close to his face and breathe them in. But most of all he wanted to embrace the old Kodak camera and feel the essence of Ernest's touch on his most loved possession.

He looked at Aimee and broke the spell.

'You said you went to Bailleul before you came to the UK. Did you visit the farmhouse?'

'Non, there is nothing left of it. I went to visit the cemetery to say thank you to Bill.'

'Did you find his grave?'

'Yes, there are rows and rows of white headstones and I realised each one of those plaques was for a young soldier like Bill and Ernest. It made me sad, but it was a beautiful crisp winter's day and the yellow roses were still in bloom. It struck me as a peaceful place to rest, shoulder to shoulder with your brave companions. I found Bill's grave. It was well kept and his headstone had a crest carved on to it, probably from his regiment. I laid some tiny purple, red and yellow winter flowers on it and thanked him for my life with all the love in my heart.'

Aimee stared out of the window. For the first time she looked sad. She swallowed and a tiny stuttered sniff escaped her nose. Raymond touched her arm.

'Come on,' he said. 'Put your coat on. One last thing. It's something Ernest showed me.'

'I don't know – it's late. I should go. I have to leave tomorrow.'

'Please,' said Raymond. 'When I met Ernest, he asked me to take a chance on him. My life has never been better since I did. Now I'm asking you to do the same with me – one small chance.' He closed his eyes, feeling the moment. 'Please.'

CHAPTER TWENTY-NINE

Learning to Fly (Part Two)

The street lights flickered, shrouded in the mist that swirled around them.

There was a hum in the air, a crackle of electricity.

Aimee and Raymond stood at the top of the gently sloping hill. The snow was falling heavily now, though for the moment the road remained clear. The snow caught in the curls of Aimee's hair, tiny white flakes in a sea of black.

Raymond looked up into the night sky. It was hard to distinguish between the stars and the snow but in that moment everything seemed right. And though the snowflakes melted on his face, icy in the light breeze, he felt warm and content. He glanced at Aimee illuminated in the pale golden streetlight. She turned, somehow sensing his gaze, and out of the darkness he heard Ernest's voice – words that must have circled the planet a million times before they chose this moment to settle on him.

In that second it was as if the moonlight existed only for her and as she turned, her pale face became framed by her long dark hair and an eternity of stars.

Aimee tilted her head and mouthed *What?* but Raymond couldn't reply. He just shook his head and watched in awe as a shooting star soared towards her, briefly lighting up the night sky before disappearing behind the waves of her hair.

'Are you ready?' he whispered. 'It's the closest you'll get to flying without leaving the ground.'

'Yes, I think so.' Aimee smiled uncertainly.

Raymond reached into his coat pocket and pulled out the franc.

'This is the franc Mira gave Ernest in the town square when he photographed the general.'

Aimee reached for it.

'No. Not yet. I'm going to roll it,' said Raymond, moving away from Aimee's outstretched hand. 'Follow it down the hill. Go as quickly as your legs will take you. Leap whenever you can. Don't stop even if you overtake it.'

Aimee shook her head, puzzled, but stood prepared, one foot slightly in front of the other, her knees bent – a reluctant competitor at a children's sports day.

Raymond swung his arm and sent the coin, in a perfect arc, rolling and bouncing down the hill.

Aimee rocked back on her heels, startled by Raymond's movement, then set off in pursuit of the franc.

Numbed by the cold air, her legs were reluctant companions but as her momentum increased, helped by the hill's gentle incline, her movements became more natural. And down the slope she went, running and leaping, as one with the snow and the stars.

Raymond watched, smiling.

A moment that would soar forever in the hallways of his heart nudged him and stung his eyes.

An old man, a friend. And how, in an act of grace and wonder, he leapt ...

EPILOGUE

A seagull flew over the rocky promontory using the thermals to glide and hover. Far below, canoeists paddled through a large natural arch as the waves washed against the rocks.

The seagull was old now, the matriarch of the flock. As a young bird she'd raced through the clouds, diving close to the rock face for no other reason than the sheer thrill of it and to taste the essence of being alive. But now she left the excitement to the youngsters and was content to glide on the warm air with only the slightest movement of her slate-grey wing tips to adjust her position.

It had been a beautiful day with a perfect blue sky, and the warmth of the sun had eased the ache of her tired old muscles.

Holidaymakers had packed the beach all day long, and she'd only ventured a couple of times to the rocks to forage for discarded chips, which over the years had become her favourite meal.

There were fewer people now, and the sun was low in the sky, sending shadows across the sand. But the breeze still whispered warm against her feathers.

She saw a family running across the beach and she glided above them to see closer. A man, slight of build, clasped a woman's hand. Her curly black hair flowed behind her as she ran. The adults held the hands of two small girls, one with long strawberry-blonde hair tied at the back, the other with shorter red hair that seemed to glow in the sun.

The seagull looked again at the man. Some far distant memory infused her wings with happiness and she swooped around them. The children laughed and pointed at her. Then the four of them, hand in hand, charged across the sand, taking a moment to wave at a man and woman sitting in deckchairs by the cliff.

The seagull used the thermals from the rock face to glide above the other couple. They were elderly and sat close to each other, their shoulders touching. They smiled and waved at the family. Strangely, they were reading the same book, his held closely to his chest as he waved, hers lying on the sand so she could use both hands to signal her delight.

The book on the beach caught in the light breeze and the pages fanned until it closed. The seagull could just make out some sunflowers on the front cover, their beautiful yellow heads entwined with many others in a sea of green and gold.

Had the seagull been able to read she would have made out the words bold against the yellow,

Cold Sunflowers by Dougal Hyland.

But, of course, she could not, and she flew into the blue sky, happy to have spent another day on this wonderful planet full of endless possibilities.

ACKNOWLEDGMENTS

With thanks to Eleanor, Louise and Averill. All my old work colleagues especially those in my teams – you kept me sane during difficult times. Everyone at Design for Writers, especially Andrew, who put up with my 3.00 a.m. changes of heart without complaint. My mum Barbara, who has helped me during the worst of times. Jean and Harry for always being in my corner. The Stanway gang (plus honourary additions) – you have no idea. Psycho Dehlia. Poppy for being Poppy. Eleanor for always smiling and always being positive and above all Penny – I could not have done it without you.

The poem read by Mira is *Surprised by Joy* by William Wordsworth, one of my favourites.

A NOTE ON THE AUTHOR

Mark Sippings was born in Walthamstow in 1959. He now lives in Essex. He has two daughters and would like a puppy.

Cold Sunflowers is his first novel.

www.coldsunflowers.co.uk
@marksipps

CPSIA information can be obtained
at www.ICGtesting.com
Printed in the USA
LVHW031116280420
654669LV00017B/1757